YONA

Deanna Irwin

Yona by Deanna Irwin. ISBN 978-1-951985-70-7 (casebound), 978-1-951985-75-2 (eBook).

Published 2020 by Virtualbookworm.com Publishing Inc., P.O. Box 9949, College Station, TX 77842, US.

CHAPTER ONE

GRIFFIN AND EDGAR CROUCHED DOWN on the cliff overlooking the native village. The two ranch hands had been crossing the plains for several months, gathering wild horses to take back to town and sell. Their employer had issued them a contract to bring in thirty stallions, and time was running short. The men were exhausted but knew full well that they could not afford not to deliver what their boss demanded. As time passed, they grew hungry and weary as their food supply ran low. After discovering this small Iroquois village, they'd decided to steal the remainder of the horses they needed, rather than track down another herd. The horses in the native village would be more than enough to fill their order and allow them to return home. So, they watched, and they waited, and tonight was their opportunity to steal the villagers' stock. The moon glistened brightly through the thick darkness of night as the last of the tribe settled down to bed. The men waited patiently until everyone was sound asleep, trying not to drift off themselves.

"Are you sure about this, Griffin?" Edgar whispered to his friend. "Maybe we ought not to be messing with these savage folk," he warned.

Griffin rolled his eyes. He was tired of talking about the plan and just wanted to steal the horses and go home. "Stop being ridiculous," he commanded.

"But Griffin, there are only two of us and so many of them. If they catch us, they could do horrible, horrible things to us. I have heard talk about how they torture and mutilate people." Griffin started making his way to the edge of the precipice. Edgar didn't budge and became desperate to stop his friend's progress. His voice got louder. "The stories also say they talk to the critters and have them attack you." Griffin shook his head in disbelief and turned back towards his friend to quiet him before he woke the natives. Edgar continued his case to try and convince his friend to walk away. "And the stories also say that they know how to use dark magic to make spells and stuff."

Griffin ran back to his friend and grabbed him by the face angrily. "For God's sake, shut up, you fool," he demanded. "We don't want to wake nobody." He took his hand off Edgar's mouth and took a step back. "Who told you these stupid stories, anyway—children?"

Edgar shook his head and opened his mouth to answer the question but stopped abruptly when Griffin lifted his hand.

"Look, I know you are scared, but what choice do we have?" He paused for a second and tilted his head, waiting for an answer. "We can go back out there in the dust and try to catch more horses, but the sun will likely kill us. Or we can go home without the full order, and the boss will definitely kill us. Or we get our butts down there, get the damn horses, and go home to a bag of money. I know what option I am choosing."

With that, he stomped off and headed down the bluff.

Edgar knew that this was their only real option, but he was scared. He had never seen the native people before, but the stories that he heard every night in the tavern gave him nightmares. He said a quick prayer asking for God's protection and followed his friend toward the village.

Griffin had heard the stories from time to time as well, and truth be told, was not crazy about getting so close to the natives either. This was not a great plan, but he needed the horses and knew that he could not survive many more days in the wild. *This should be simple enough*, he reminded himself. *We climb down the side of this rock, sneak up to the herd, and slowly lead them up that path. Hopefully, by the time they are missed, we will be halfway back to town.*

In the few minutes that it took them to make their way halfway into their journey, a strange, dark cloud began to cover the moon. The sky was growing dark very quickly. "How can that be?" he asked. "The entire sky was clear just a moment ago. Where did the clouds come from?" He took a few more steps and stopped abruptly. A low growl rumbled through the air. He stood frozen in place. And then another slow, rumbling growl echoed through the hills. *Is that thunder?* Both men held their breath for a moment to quietly listen. Neither made a sound. The third growl sounded like it came from directly behind them, and both men began to shake. Griffin spun around to see what was about to attack them. "What was that, a mountain lion?" he whispered to Edgar. "Maybe it is a badger?"

Edgar was too scared to answer. He just shook his head repeatedly. Griffin thought he heard another growl behind him and spun around again. This time his footing slipped, he lost his balance, and he fell backwards, grabbing the rock face. He slid down the rock face, bouncing from boulder to boulder until his body landed at the bottom in a lifeless heap.

Edgar was in shock. He stood as still as a statue, too frightened to move. His chest was so tight, he struggled even to get air into his lungs. He repeatedly gasped in panic, trying to force enough air into his lungs to be able to shout. Finally, he got out a word: "Griff!" He continued to gasp, trying to force his lungs to open. He had never been so scared in all his life. "Griffin, you hurt?" he yelled.

Again, a low growl shook the night. Edgar crouched down and tried to hide. *What kind of critter could be stalking on the side of a cliff*? he wondered. The night had grown pitch black by now, and he could not see a thing. He looked up to the sky to try and find the moon, to get his bearings. He had to make it back to the camp so he could get out of there. "Griffin," he yelled again desperately, hoping that his friend would answer. He looked down and was surprised that he could see the village. He couldn't make his way around the bluff, but he could still see the village. It was quiet and peaceful. It actually calmed him down a bit. Maybe he was just hearing things; maybe it was his own fear creating sounds in his head. He stared at the village for a moment. His heart began to slow down. Breathing became a little easier. He was developing some hope. Maybe he could find his way back and make it home. He turned to move toward the top of the cliff. A few steps up, he felt the sensation of hot breath brushing across the back of his neck. He stopped and spun around. *Where is that coming from*? Another growl rumbled past him. His heart was pounding once again. Then he felt the breath on his face. It was the worst stench he had ever encountered. Whatever was stalking him was right in front of him now. He could not move, he could not breathe; his body shook violently in fear. He closed his eyes tightly and waited for an attack. When nothing happened, he raised his hand out in front of his face to find the origin of the breath. *What is this beast*? Feeling like his heart was about to burst out of his chest, Edgar finally found the courage to run. He turned and climbed the bluff as fast as he could. When he'd almost reached the top, he heard another long growl. This time it sounded like it was right next to his ear. He pushed hard to get his body over the top edge and jumped to his feet. Suddenly, something grabbed him from behind. Fierce claws dug into both his shoulders. The pain was excruciating as the beast picked him up twenty feet into the air, let out a thunderous growl, and threw him across the dirt with such force that his body bounced when it hit the ground.

Edgar's body was broken, and the pain was so overwhelming that he was barely conscious, but he was determined to make his way back to safety. It took all the energy he had to roll over onto his stomach so he could begin to pull himself across the dirt. His broken legs dragged behind him, leaving a trail of blood. Another growl pierced the night. He fell limp into the dirt. He rolled onto his back and lay there, motionless, hoping the beast would think he was dead. The awful stench of breath returned. It was directly in his face again. He knew there was no more hope. He closed his eyes and waited for death to come. He felt the jagged teeth tear into his neck, and then the pain stopped as he slipped into the darkness.

CHAPTER TWO

In the early days of the United States, long before the Revolutionary War and the Declaration of Independence, English settlers were struggling to build a new life along the Eastern coast, and many divergent tribes of natives were scattered throughout the west.

For many generations, the Iroquois nation inhabited the northern woodlands of what is now known as the state of Ohio. They were not an aggressive people. They were peaceful farmers who grew crops, hunted, and taught their children to respect nature and the earth around them. Iroquois shaman used plants and nature to create powerful medicines. They respected the earth and were grateful for the bounty it supplied their people. They planted more than they reaped, only killed for food, and built shrines to show respect for the earth and to honor their ancestors. Tales of the Iroquois tribe's mighty magic spread throughout the region as they passed their recipes and secrets down from generation to generation.

When the warrior tribes of the west began to move into the valley close to their home, the Iroquois were faced with a life-changing choice to make. Did they stay and defend their homeland against the violent enemy tribes, or flee to the east and the south? They had weapons, but only for hunting, not enough to defend themselves from the brutal violence of the warrior western tribes.

After praying to the elders for many moons, one night the tribal leader had a vision that told him to travel with his people east for two winters, until they came to a smaller river. When they arrive at the river, they would be greeted by a large flock of great birds. There they could rebuild their village safely and live out their days in peace, hidden from the violence of the warring nations that were closing in on them. The tribal elders knew that the journey would be long and dangerous but agreed that it was best for their young, so that is exactly what they did.

Mahoog was very young when her people packed up all that they could carry and began the long journey east. She spent a large portion of her childhood helping her tribe move to their new home. The journey was neither quick nor easy. Along the way, they lost beloved family members to sickness and old age, but the tribe of thousands remained strong. Mahoog's mother was a healer and tended to the people of the tribe. Mahoog assisted her mother in caring for the wounded, delivering babies, and preparing the dead for burial. She was learning how to make medicines, chant healing prayers, and cast healing spells. Her mother was teaching her the ways that were passed down to her from her mother, and Mahoog prayed that someday she would be able to pass the knowledge down to her own daughter. Mahoog often wondered if they would ever find the land that the vision had promised them, but her mother never lost faith. At night, they would sit by the fire and talk about the life they would have by the river with the birds. Mahoog's mother noticed her daughter's attention often turning toward a certain young hunter and knew that it would not be long before Mahoog was sitting at the evening fire with her own children.

Darkness had begun to come earlier, and the winds were getting colder. The tribe knew that winter was once again approaching. They had hoped to find the new home before another winter set in upon them. The journey had taken them almost through what would someday become known as Pennsylvania. It has been such a long trek. The tribe was beginning to grow weak, and some were losing faith. As the sun began to set across the hills and they were getting ready to make camp for the night, a scout announced that he heard rushing water up ahead. Excited, the people decided to travel just a bit farther. As the first of the group climbed up a large hill, they too heard the water. The excitement drove them to move faster. As soon as they crested the next hill, they saw it. There, on a low branch, was a beautiful brown breasted hawk—and then another one, and another one. As they ran toward the river, the birds seemed to be in every tree along its banks. They let out loud cries to alert the rest of the tribe. They finally had found it, the smaller river with the great birds. They had found their new home, the envisioned river, their promised land.

They named the river *Susquehanna* and lived happily along its peaceful banks in the land where the Amish now live, hidden from the ferocious western warrior tribes for generations. Mahoog did have a daughter and taught her the secret healing magic long used by her people. Mahoog's daughter then taught her daughter, who went on to teach *her* daughter.

Mahoog's great-great-granddaughter, Assomaha, had lost her own mother at a young age but had learned enough from her to become the tribe healer as well. Like many of the generations before her, she anxiously awaited the day that she could teach her own daughter. She spent her days tending to the village sick and elderly. In the evenings, she often wandered through the fields gathering plants and herbs to make medicines for her patients. She very much enjoyed taking care of her people but longed for the day she would have her own children to take care of as well.

Across the village, Natick looked out over the pastures watching her mate, the tribal chief, and their son Uzumati chasing one another with long grass switches. *Look at them*, she thought to herself, *they are supposed to be gathering and are playing around like small children.* Uzumati had grown into a fine young man who now stood taller than his great father. Natick hoped that one day soon, her son would discover one of the available young maidens in the tribe and start a family of his own. So far, it did not appear to her that he had even noticed that any of the young girls in the tribe had grown into beautiful young women.

They noticed him, though. After all, he was the chief's son, tall and handsome, brave and somewhat loud at times. From the time he could walk, Uzumati worked hard to impress his father and anyone else that was in the vicinity. He pushed to be faster, stronger, and braver than the other bucks, for one day he would succeed his father as chief and be fully responsible for leading his tribe and keeping them safe. Natick knew that someday he would choose a bride and give her the grandchildren she was longing for. But as she watched the two men cracking each other with the wheatgrass, leaving thick red welts across each other's bodies, she knew that today was not likely to be that day. She shook her head and returned to her own work.

Natick and the chief were both very proud of their only son. He was a kind soul, but was also strong and cunning. He was a talented hunter and worked hard to provide food for the entire village. However, Natick was slightly disappointed each night when her son returned to his parents' hut. She would sigh as she realized, night after night, that today was not the day he had met his true love. She was often tempted to push her son to talk to girls but knew that it was not a mother's place. One afternoon while cleaning a basket of corn, she did mention her desires to her mate, hoping that perhaps he could hurry their boy along somehow.

"Mother," the chief replied, "give the boy some time. Anyone can wrestle a coyote, but only the bravest of warriors can wrangle a woman. They can be quite ferocious." Then he laughed.

Natick didn't appreciate his joke and threw the cob of corn she was cleaning at him playfully.

"See what I mean?" he joked. "He will start a family as his destiny is written. You must just be patient, my love."

"I am patient, but I would like to hold my grandchildren before I return to the earth." Uzumati came in and sat down next to her, so she dropped the conversation. She smiled at her son, watching him adjust the string on his bow. *If only you would pay as much attention to a girl as you do that thing,* she thought as she returned to her chore.

Then one summer night, it did happen. Uzumati did not return to his parents' hut before they drifted off to sleep. It was a very warm night, but a strong, cool wind was whistling through the village. The moon was full and bright. Uzumati decided to climb to the top of the bluff to get a better view for a while. As he made his way up the rock, the wind pushed at him, and he almost lost his footing several times. It went through his head what a stupid thing he was doing. *I should just go back down to bed,* he thought, but somehow the light of the moon was calling to him, so he continued his climb. Carefully he worked himself up the steep wall, rock by rock, as the dirt crumbled under his fingertips. When he finally reached the top, he pulled himself onto the edge and lay on his back in the dirt for a few minutes to catch his breath. Lying there panting, he wondered how he was going to make his way back down.

He relaxed for a few moments, the warm breeze brushing across his body. He listened to the night sounds—crickets chirping, whippoorwills cooing, and in the distance, he heard a large owl calling out to its mate. It was very relaxing, and he nearly drifted off to sleep. Then suddenly, there was something else. There was something lovely drifting on the breeze. He heard a soft voice singing. At first he thought it was a dove, and then perhaps the song of an angel. He sat up and turned around. At first, all Uzumati could see was the giant moon shining brightly on the horizon. As his eyes began to focus, he could make out the silhouette of a woman swaying side to side with the wind. Her dance was graceful, and her song was soothing. He recognized her from the village, he had known her all his life, but he'd never noticed how beautiful she had grown. *How could he not,* he thought as he sat memorized. Finally, he called out to her: "Assomaha."

The sudden voice startled her. At first she was angry at the interruption, and then she was curious at how he found her secret location. Feeling intruded upon, she grabbed her shawl and wrapped it tightly around her as she flopped down on a log. "Uzumati, what are you doing up here?" she snapped. "Why aren't you asleep?" Still admiring how lovely she looked, he did not answer. He arose and dusted the dirt from his legs, and then made his way to where she was sitting and joined her. Realizing that he had not walked past her, she wondered how he'd made his way to the top of the cliff. "Wait a minute; did you climb up the rocks? You could have been killed!"

Confused, he nodded sheepishly. "How did you come?"

"There is a path around the back side of the rocks," she laughed. "You have lived in the village all of your life. How did you not know that?" They both laughed. Then there was silence. Uzumati awkwardly attempted to begin a conversation several times. He was nervous and not comfortable talking to a girl. She sensed his uneasiness and helped him along. Eventually, they began to relax and enjoy the company. Before they knew it, the moon had faded behind the mountains, and the sun was beginning to peek over the opposite horizon.

The two became inseparable after that night, and when the earth turned brown and the trees prepared for snow, the young couple was wed. Natick was never as happy as she was at that moment.

When the snow had disappeared, and the crops began to grow once again, the young couple received another wonderful surprise. Assomaha was scooping water from the river when she felt it. At first, she wasn't quite sure. She dropped the pail and stood straight with her hand on her belly. *Could it really be?* she thought to herself. And then it happened again: movement. She knew she was with child, and tears of joy flowed rampantly down her face. She ran back to her hut so fast, she did not realize that her water buckets were floating away. Over and over she called for her husband. He thought something was wrong and ran to her side in a panic. She could not find the words through her tears of joy, so she simply grabbed his hand and placed it on her stomach. His eyes almost popped out of his head when he too felt the movement and knew that they were about to have a family. He hugged his wife tightly, and then ran around the village yipping in joy, letting everyone in on the news.

Through her entire pregnancy, Uzumati took special care of his wife. Almost every day he would make another gift for the son he expected to have. Today, he presented her with a tiny bow and arrows. He could not wait to teach the boy to be a great hunter like his father.

The leaves had turned to color by the time the baby finally arrived. Darkness crept in early this time of year, and the sun had already set by the time Assomaha had finished making dinner for her husband. As she cleaned up after the meal and began to ready for bed, she could feel the pains beginning and knew the baby was ready to meet its parents. Holding her large belly with one hand, she smiled at her husband and softly ran her other hand down his cheek. Then she disappeared into their hut. Her mate summoned the elder women of the tribe, and then sat by the fire to wait for his son. Natick ran to aid in the birth of her eagerly awaited grandchild. She was so excited that her feet barely touched the ground. She grabbed Uzumati and hugged him tightly then disappeared into the hut to help with the birth.

Assomaha was the medicine giver of the tribe, so it was normally her job to deliver the babies. She knew that the elders would be there to comfort her, but most of the work would still fall to her. As she leaned back onto a pile of animal hides, she saw the tiny bear skin papoose that her man had made to keep the baby warm. Months prior, he had discovered the carcass of a great black bear along the hunting trail. He brought the hide back to the village, tanned it on the warm rocks during the hottest days of the summer, and then spent hours cutting and stitching it into a perfect little pocket for his child.

The moon was enormous over the camp that night. It was so big and red, it appeared that the sky was on fire. The fearless hunter sat for hours and watched as the moon moved across the sky. As he listened to the commotion inside his home, he felt helpless for the first time in his life. He kicked at the dirt and worried for his wife. Surely, he thought, she would be alright. This bright, full moon must be a sign from the spirits that she would be alright. After all, Assomah meant moon. He thought of the night they spent on the hill under the same moon and could almost hear her soft voice floating on the night breeze once again.

Just as the bottom edge of the great moon touched the top of the farthest mountain, Natick emerged from the hut and smiled at her son. He shot to his feet, anxiously waiting for news. She handed him what looked like a ball of blanket. He slowly pulled back the corner to see a tiny set of eyes looking back at him. *This is the most beautiful face I have ever seen,* he thought to himself. The great hunter felt tears stream down his tough face. He opened the blanket the rest of the way to see his son for the first time. It was then that he discovered his much-anticipated son was actually a girl.

He stood confused for a moment. It never crossed his mind, even once, that the baby could be a girl. He chuckled to himself but was not disappointed. He held the tiny baby with both hands and raised her above his head toward the bright moon to thank the spirits for this amazing gift. Then he whooped a loud war cry in celebration of his excitement that woke half of the village. He ran to his wife and fell next to her on the skins, placing the baby on her chest and hugging her tightly. The family was so happy but also exhausted. They drifted off together, dreaming of the many children they hoped would follow this beautiful little girl.

CHAPTER THREE

LIFE ALONG THE SUSQUEHANNA RIVER was peaceful, and the tribe grew in numbers as the years went by. The more aggressive warrior tribes did not venture this far east, and the village was careful to avoid the white settlers that were now moving into the area surrounding them.

Assomaha's family spent every moment loving and nurturing their beautiful new daughter. They named her Xuan (Sue Ann), which means "wise bird," after the hawks that led her people to their wonderful new home many years ago. Xuan could barely walk when her mother began teaching her how to harness the power of nature to heal and protect the tribe. The girl was smart, and happy, and strong. Her father took her into the woods and taught her about the plants and animals that lived there. He also took her hunting, so that she would be able to provide for her own family someday. In the evening, they would play so hard that Xuan would often laugh herself to sleep. At the end of their daughter's sixth winter, Assomaha felt her second child beginning to grow inside of her. The spirits had blessed her little family generously. Life was good.

As Assomaha's belly grew and she prepared for her new baby's arrival, trouble came to the village. People began to disappear. Hunting parties would return missing a few members, and the tribal leaders became fearful for the safety of their people. Women would go into the hills to gather for the tribe and not return. Search parties would find nothing. Her people were very careful to avoid the light-skinned towns that were now spreading like wild fire. Assomaha knew in her heart that these people had begun to attack her people and feared that they would eventually try to push them from this land. Once again, this peaceful race of people had to decide whether to fight back against the attackers that threatened their home, or to move on. Her people were not warriors; they did not know how to create war or to defend themselves from the weapons of the white man. They prayed to the spirits for guidance and protection. Assomaha just could not understand why the spirits would bring them to this land, and then take it away from them. Surely the tribe could not leave this place, but she felt the darkness that the future held for them if they did not. She stroked her daughter's long hair and wondered if her children would have the opportunity to grow up to have their own children someday.

The tribe did not speak of the danger that they all knew the white man brought to their people. They made excuses for the disappearances and pretended that the new settlers were not closing in on the land around their village. Every time the hunters went into the forest, Assomaha would pray to the spirits to protect them and bring her husband back to her safely.

It would only be a matter of time before the white settlers came into their camp, like they had done to so many others. On the night of the third full moon of the next harvest season, Assomaha's worst fears came true. Riders came to her village in the middle of the night while everyone was asleep. The men of the tribe had no time to react or do anything to protect their people. The attackers came bursting into the camp, firing their guns at anything that moved and burning every home they came upon. Women were screaming, children crying, and there was so much confusion as families ran to find each other, trying to escape the commotion. Thick black smoke filled the village as the hides covering the homes began to burn. The smell was overwhelming.

Assomaha woke with a jolt. She could not find her husband and was terrified. She crawled across the tent floor and woke her daughter. She grabbed a blanket to wrap around Xuan's shoulders and took her tiny, trembling hand into her own. They were going to have to run to the forest if they were going to escape these terrible people. She crept over to the opening and peeped out. There were men on horseback everywhere she looked. They were riding through the village, swinging their hatchets and torches. All of the teepees surrounding hers were already on fire, and the screams of her dying family made her sick to her stomach. She looked down at her swollen belly. She knew she was much too far along with her second child to be able to run away. A tear streamed down her cheek. *I have to do something,* she thought. *I have to save my daughter.*

She hunched down in front of the girl and placed both hands on her tiny head. She tilted her head backwards as if to absorb the power of the moon that was shining in through an opening at the top of the tent. She began to chant as quickly as she could. She knew that she only had seconds before her daughter was going to have to make a run for the trees behind their teepee, but she was desperately trying to finish placing a protection spell on the girl to help her get away. She chanted and sang, and asked the great spirits to protect her child and help her to escape this nightmare.

Xuan was so scared. She tried pulling on her mother's arm, wanting them both to run away. The screams were coming closer and the smoke was getting thick, making it hard to breathe. Her eyes burned and she was confused. *What was her mother saying? Why wasn't she running?* Then suddenly everything went silent for a moment, and Xuan felt something wet hit her face. Assomaha stopped chanting and gasped for air. Her face turned white, and she looked into Xuan's eyes, "Run, baby girl, run away," she said as her hands fell from the girl's head. Xuan looked down and saw an arrowhead pushed out of her mother's chest. She screamed and stepped back, crying hysterically. "I love you," Assomaha whispered as she collapsed forward on to the ground.

"Mama, get up," she pleaded as she pulled on her mother's arm. She didn't know what else to do. She was so scared that she could not even think. Then, through the tear the arrow made in the teepee before it struck her mother, Xuan saw flames starting to engulf her home. The fear took over and she turned to run. Her heart pounded and her head was throbbing. She did not know where to go, but she ran directly through the chaos toward the river. The trees would give her a place to hide, if she could make it that far. One of the attackers saw the little girl dart out of the teepee and kicked his horse hard to chase after her. No one was going to get away tonight. The little girl squealed and ducked under a wooden table, and bolted out the other side. The horse could not maneuver through the camp as fast as the tiny girl who lived there. Finally making it to the edge of the forest, she pushed her way into the thick brush, where no horse could follow. The disappointed man paced his animal back and forth for a moment, considering his options. He waved his torch to light the darkness and allow him to see through the trees. He did not want to let her get away but was not about to dismount and follow her into the dark. After all, her people were savages. She could have a weapon.

Xuan crouched down, hiding for a few moments, trying not to make a sound but still sobbing hysterically. Once she was sure the man had returned to the village, she got up and ran as fast as she could in the other direction, deeper into the forest. Her heart was pounding so hard, it felt as though it would explode out of her chest. The woodland carpet hurt her feet and branches continued to slap at her as she pushed through the thick brush, desperate to escape. She quickly lost her breath and the pain became hard to bear, but every time she began to slow down, she heard more gunshots and screams from her village and continued to push on further. Finally, too exhausted to go on, she came to the river—the same river that had promised her tribe the safety of a new home—and collapsed beside a large rock. Trembling in fear, she pushed her little body as far under the rock as she could fit and passed out.

In the morning, when the sun finally pried the little girl's eyes open, she once again began to cry. Her feet were torn up from the sticks and rocks that she ran over the night before. Her dress was torn and dirty. She tried to wipe it clean with her hands and cried harder when she could not. Climbing up on top of the rock, she sat for a moment, not knowing what to do. She did not know the way to her village and was far too afraid of the white invaders to even attempt to find her way home. She remembered her mother falling to the floor in front of her. She cried out "Mama" and began crying hysterically once again. She laid her head on the warm rock and cried herself back to sleep.

A few hours had passed when Xuan had once again woken up. This time it was her rumbling stomach that woke her. She knew she had to find something to eat but did not know where to look. She bent down next to the water's edge to get a drink. She cupped her hands together and lifted water to her mouth several times to drink, and then splashed the water on her face. The cool water felt good on the scratches that painted her face. She decided to slip her bloody feet into the water as well. After a few minutes, the pain was relieved enough for her to begin walking. She did not know where to go, so she began following the river uphill. She remembered her father telling her that the white man came from down the river, and she was desperate to get as far away from them as she could. She slowly made her way through the thick brush with her tummy still growling and tears streaming down her little cheeks.

When the sun was directly over her head and very hot, she picked a large leaf and placed it on her head for shade. Out of the corner of her eye, she saw a woman duck behind a tree. Excitedly thinking that she was no longer alone, she ran toward the tree, but when she got there she could not find anyone. She spun around looking in every direction. She was sure she saw someone. Then in a whisper, she heard her mother's voice. "Xuan" she called.

"Mama," the little girl screamed. Could it really be? Xuan excitedly ran toward where she thought the voice was coming from.

"Mama, mama," she called out again and again.

"Xuan," the voice whispered again changing the girl's direction. Several more times, the whisper called her name, leading her through the forest. Finally, the tiny girl pushed through a wall of foliage and saw a giant bush full of large, ripe, ruby-colored berries. She giggled loudly and grabbed a fist full to plunge into her mouth. She ate berries until her belly was hard and her hands were as red as rubies. Then she nestled into a pile of leaves and once again went to sleep.

The little girl spent the next few days wandering between the river for water and her giant berry bush. She played in the forest during the day and buried herself in the leaves at night. She would dream of her village and the people who loved her. She was happy in her dreams, and then awoke each morning to the loneliness of her new world and cried. One night she was dreaming that she was walking through the meadow with her mother. She thanked her mother for finding her the berry tree.

"I will always take care of you, my love," her mother reassured her. Then she bent down and placed her hands upon Xuan's cheeks. "But you cannot stay here. You must keep walking."

Xuan awoke suddenly and understood the message from her mother. The berries had begun to make the little girl's stomach ache, and she knew that she needed to find a safer place to be. She picked the biggest leaf that she could find and filled it with berries to carry with her. She went to the river for a quick drink of water, and then set out once again on her journey to find a new home.

Xuan pressed on, following the river north. At times the brush would become so dense that she had to get down on her knees and crawl through it. She stopped every few hours to eat a few of the berries. She was scared and alone. She cried for her mother many times throughout each day. As each day passed, she became weaker and weaker.

As the sun began to set on yet another day alone, Xuan saw a large bird circling the sky, high above the trees. She watched it flying gracefully through the air, around and around. She spun around so the majestic bird could not get out of her sight. It was then that she heard her mother's whisper once again.

"Follow," she whispered.

Just then, as if the bird knew the girl understood the command, it stopped circling and began to fly north. Xuan followed the bird for almost an hour. Every time she slowed down and thought about stopping, her guide let out a frightening screech, as if to coach her onward. After a while longer, the bird perched high in a tree, and the little girl collapsed on the forest floor for a nap.

When she awoke, night had fallen and the woods were once again pitch black. Her new friend was still perched in the tree, watching over her. She rubbed her eyes, and then her growling belly. She was so hungry. All of a sudden, the breeze changed direction and brought her a different smell. It smelled like smoke. Following the smell through the thick trees, she could see a small campfire in a clearing up ahead. Her heart was pounding. *What if it is the awful people that hurt my mother?* she wondered. She wanted to run away, but she smelled food. She just had to see where it was coming from. Slowly she crept forward. Trembling in fear, she crouched down very low to peek into the camp. There was only one old man sitting by the fire. He was talking loudly, but there was no one else with him. The little girl did not understand. *Who was this crazy old man talking to?* Then she saw it. Hanging over the fire was a fat rabbit fastened to a spit, cooking over the flames. She almost cried out loud. She was so hungry and had not eaten anything more than leaves and berries for days. Somehow, she had to get that rabbit.

Quietly, Xuan circled around the old miner's camp to the other side. Creeping very slowly as the man sang loudly by his fire, being very careful as to not make a sound, she reached up and untied the man's mule that was grazing a few feet from the camp. As she began to back away, the mule looked at her and let out a very loud bray.

"Eee-awww," the creature bellowed.

This startled Xuan so much that she fell backward, breaking twigs as she hit the ground hard. Scared that the man had heard her and would be coming, she rolled up in a tight ball and wrapped her arms around her head.

"Shut up, you old nag," the man yelled. "There is nothing wrong with my singing."

Relieved that the man did not come over to see where the noise came from, the tiny girl crawled back around the camp halfway to the other side. Then she picked up a rock and hurled it as hard as she could at the mule, hitting it square in the hindquarters. The animal screamed out once again and took off running into the darkness.

Eee-awww, eee-awww, eee-awww, it bellowed as it disappeared into the night.

"Dag nabbit, you blasted animal," the man yelled as he jumped to his feet. He threw his whiskey bottle to the ground and took off to catch his mule. He too disappeared into the darkness, but Xuan could hear him cursing through the forest. That's when she knew it was safe to make her move. She ran into the camp and grabbed the stick holding the juicy rabbit over the fire. It was hot, but there was no way she was going to give up her prize. She began to run away and then stopped. She went back to where the old man had been sitting. Wrapping her dress around her hand so she would not get burned, she tore off a piece of the meat and laid it on the large rock. That way when the man returned, he could have something to eat as well. Then she quietly slipped off into the darkness to find a place to devour her feast.

The rabbit tasted wonderful, and Xuan could not get enough. She hurriedly ate as much as she could. It had been days since she'd had any protein. When every scrap of meat was off the bones and her belly was once again big and hard, the little girl lay back in the tall grass and fell asleep.

The old miner finally caught up to his renegade mule and led him back to the campsite. After tying him up securely, he was ready for his supper. Imagine his disappointment when he noticed that his entree had disappeared.

"Darn coyotes," he yelled as he kicked the rock that he had been sitting on. "This is your fault, you stubborn old beast."

And then he saw the meat Xuan had left on the rock for him. No animal would leave a scrap that big behind. Confused, he picked up the meat and smelled it. He did not know how smelling it could determine if it was still safe to eat or not, but he did it anyway. He was so hungry, he just ate it. Wiping his hands on his dusty pants, he grabbed a branch and dipped it into the fire. Using the burning stick as a lantern, he searched the ground around his campfire. There in the dirt, he saw the tiny foot prints that Xuan had left behind.

I knew it weren't no animal that stole my rabbit, he thought to himself, but what in tar-nation is a child doing out here in the wilderness?

He decided to get a good night's sleep and set out to track the thief at first light. The moment the first few rays of sunlight began to peek over the horizon, the miner packed up to begin tracking his new prey.

Xuan slept well for a few hours, and then the same nightmare about the day she lost her mother once again jolted her awake with a scream. Shaking, she rubbed her eyes and headed to the river to wash off the sticky remains of her dinner the night before. After a few minutes at the river, her bird friend swooped down out of the sky with a loud screech. The little girl knew that it was time to go and quickly began once again to follow her guide through the forest. She was growing weaker and very much wanted to lie back down and sleep. All of a sudden, she heard the same whinny from the night before.

"Eeeee-awwww!"

Oh, no, the old man is coming. In a state of panic, she took off running as fast as her little body could handle. Once again, her feet were getting torm up by the rough ground of the wilderness. She ran until her breath grew heavy and her sight grew dark. She began crying uncontrollably. She stopped on the edge of a small clearing, gasping to try and get some air into her lungs. Her chest was pounding and her head was spinning. Stabbing pains cramped her stomach as she bent forward searching for some relief. After a few more pants, dehydration and exhaustion overwhelmed her tiny body, and Xuan fell to the ground.

The miner continued to follow his prey. He was intrigued as he followed the little footprints carefully, searching for signs that they were accompanied by an adult. He pushed on, knowing that he was getting close. The brush was very thick, but he heard movement on the other side of a large row of bushes. He waited silently for a moment and heard another twig snap. Then he noticed a small opening in the bush line, where he was sure his little thief must have pushed through. He smiled profusely. He had her now. He quietly tied his mule to a branch and bent his old bones down to his knees. Pushing aside the thorny bush, he squeezed his body through the brush. Once through, he jumped to his feet in hopes of scaring his prey.

But it was he that was surprised. His jaw dropped open and he stood for a moment, not believing his eyes. A few feet in front of him stood the largest black bear he had ever seen. She was angry and howled a long, fierce growl at the man. He began to shake. The bear pushed hard on her front paws and stood erect to once again chastise the man for being there. This time he could feel her hot breath on his face. He wrapped his hands around his head and cowered to the ground. She continued to growl at him. Turning his feet toward the monster, he used his legs to push himself back through the opening of the bushes. Once on the other side, he moved as fast as lighting to untie the mule and ride away.

The bear did not follow the old man. She just wanted him to leave. She turned toward Xuan and sniffed her a few times. She poked at the girl with her snout, pushing her a few feet across the dirt. When the girl remained motionless, the bear snorted at her. Then the animal gathered the back of Xuan's dress in her huge jaws and used it to lift the child.

She carried the toddler for hours, with her little arms and legs dragging though the dirt and brush. Xuan was groggy and barely regained consciousness for a few moments at a time. She was awake enough to open her eyes, but not enough to understand what was happening. She imagined that she could hear the drums of her village and her people chanting. She thought she was at home with her mother, sleeping in her bed. When the bear laid her softly on the ground to rest, Xuan opened her eyes and looked up at the great bear.

"Yona," she whispered and touched the bear's face. Her father often told her stories of the great protector bear that watched over their people. They called her Yona. Then Xuan lost her battle to stay awake once again and slipped back into her exhaustion. Sensing the child was getting weaker, the bear lifted the child and hurried on her way.

After another hour, the bear came upon a clearing where several cabins had recently been built. The bear knew of this small village and had visited it before to scavenge for food. She took Xuan onto the back porch of the center cabin. She knew other children lived there. She laid the child down softly next to the door and began to walk away. Looking back at the girl, she decided to gather a few large leaves and cover the girl to keep her warm. When she got to edge of the forest, she stood on her hind legs and growled as loud as she could, hoping to get the attention of the people who lived in the house. She needed them to find the girl and help her right away. She watched as the curtain slowly pulled back, and a tiny face appeared at the bottom of the pane. Then, slowly, the door creaked open. She knew her package would be discovered and quickly disappeared back into the dark forest. Her mission was complete.

CHAPTER FOUR

JUST NORTH OF XUAN'S VILLAGE, along the same river, was a small town of Quaker settlers who were also struggling to create a safe place for their people to call home in a new world.

Sarah Ingram's family had only recently arrived in the Susquehanna Valley. Sarah and her brother were the first generation of her family born in this new country. She lived only a few miles away from the tribe, and yet still existed in a totally divergent world altogether. Her Quaker grandparents had traveled to this new land from Europe. Her grandfather had dreams of building a church in this new world and mentoring the spiritual needs of his congregation. Her father had followed in his footsteps and inherited the church and congregation upon Grandfather's retirement. Sarah and her brother Robert were raised in the church, and Robert dreamed of the day he would take his turn at the pulpit.

Life in the developing new world was not always as easy as the settlers imagined it would be. It seemed as though winters were growing longer and harder every year, and after a string of long, cold storms, Sarah's family fell on tough times. Their small town was struggling to provide enough food for all the families who lived there. Sarah's father worried that his congregation would starve, but they simply did not have the money to afford passage back to the old country. He prayed nightly for his flock. He asked his God to show them how to grow more food. He asked Him to grant them the strength to endure yet another harsh winter. And he asked for guidance on how to lead his congregation through the toughest times.

After another big storm had blanketed the land with a deep layer of snow, just as things looked the most dismal for his town, a rancher from the next town came to visit the reverend. The rancher was doing very well in the new country. He owned a vast amount of farmland and employed many hands to tend to it. He owned a thousand head of livestock that provided an endless supply of milk and meat. He came to offer the desperate man a proposal to save his people.

"Allow your daughter to marry my son, and we will feed the town through winter, and teach them to farm in the spring," the farmer suggested.

The farmer's son was rough and raw and was by no means proper husband material. The reverend prayed for guidance once again. Although it broke both his and his wife's hearts to sentence their only daughter to such a marriage, the town simply had no other options for survival. He knew this was what had to be done. Sarah married the farmer's son, Ivan, the next Sunday. It was a loveless marriage, and she was miserable, but she took comfort knowing that her neighbors were provided for. Although this was not the storybook life she'd dreamed of while growing up, there were far worse things that could have happened, she imagined.

Sarah gave Ivan two sons who became her entire world. Ivan spent his days working his father's farm and his nights at the saloon with his rowdy friends. Sarah spent every waking moment doting on her young children. They made her very happy. Ivan was not a good father, but at very least, his money would provide for them throughout their lives.

Over the years, the town grew and Sarah's father's congregation flourished. They had developed their farming skills and could provide for all the families throughout each winter. They built a school house and expanded the church. Their lives were simple, peaceful, and happy.

Travelers through the small town brought violent stories from the west about the native villagers attacking new settlements and travelers. They told such horrible tales of massacres. These stories were unsettling, even though no one in the town had ever seen a native act with any sort of aggression. The Iroquois villages that were scattered throughout the nearby land were quiet and hidden. They kept to themselves and avoided all contact with the white settlers. Surely, they could not be responsible for the violent atrocities that these travelers spoke of.

Sarah's husband, Ivan, spent most of his evenings at the local tavern drinking and listening to the drunken men tell tall tales about made-up adventures. The more he listened, and the more he drank, the more he idolized these rough and rugged adventurers. Little did he know that they were simple farmers like him during the day, and only told stories to make their lives seem more exciting than the normal long-term family life. Ivan believed their stories and hung on every word, wishing that he too could travel around, meet exotic people, and experience death-defying events. He listened each night and drank until he could barely stay awake, and then staggered home to his wife and children, passing out as soon as he got in the door.

Many nights, the wild stories included the storyteller fighting in the war against the savage natives to the west. Each man took his turn creating ridiculous stories of the supposed strange behavior of the tribes they encountered, and how savage these people were toward the newcomers. Their stories always included how the warriors ruthlessly attacked innocent groups of people, and how the heroes had to fight back to eliminate the natives and barely escaped with their lives. Ivan drank, listened, and believed these tales. As each night passed, he became more and more prejudiced toward the natives. The problem was that most of the new settlers believed these wild stories and were becoming very fearful of anyone who did not live in their small towns. The prejudice against the natives was spreading quickly throughout the new settlements. The false stories meant to bolster individual men's reputations created panic that at any moment, savages would attack the town and kill everyone who lived there. The settlers began to demand that the town leaders do something to protect them from the impending danger that was certain from these strange native people.

Ivan and his drunken comrades picked up their weapons and began patrolling the lands that surrounded their town. Drunken, armed men who are afraid of anyone that they do not recognize walking through the forest at night can only lead to trouble, and soon it did.

Meanwhile, Sarah stayed very close with her family. Ivan was not home very much, and he did not seem to mind that she loaded the boys into the wagon every weekend and traveled home to stay with her parents and brother. After her father's sermon on Sundays, Sarah would cook dinner for her family while her brother, Robert, took the boys outside to play. Week after week, they headed outside to conquer some new sort of adventure just outside the house in the backyard. Sarah sometimes wished that the boys' father would spend as much time with them as Uncle Robert did. After dinner, Grandpa would read the bible to the boys while Sarah and Robert spent hours talking. She enjoyed her weekend visits so much that it was harder each week to make the journey back home to her father-in-law's ranch.

As Sarah's belly began to swell with her third son, Ivan insisted that her attendant, Ira, begin making the trips with the family each weekend. This weekend, Ira and Sarah loaded the wagon with fresh-picked pumpkins. They planned on making pies for the church to distribute to the congregation. Ira had a secret family recipe that was simply amazing. As Sarah pulled the wagon behind the church, she called out to Robert to come help unload the supplies. When he didn't respond, Sarah's oldest boy jumped from the wagon and shouted, "I will get Uncle Robert," as he excitedly ran up the sidewalk toward the church door. Suddenly they heard loud shouting, and the boy stopped in his tracks. He turned and looked to his mother for guidance. Sarah listened for a moment but could not hear what the commotion was about. She slowly slid the door open and peered around the edge to see who was arguing. She found her father and brother in a very heated disagreement.

As soon as her father saw her, he nodded to Robert "Very good, Sarah is here. Maybe she can talk some sense into you." Then he pushed past her and stomped out of the church to help the boys unload the wagon.

"Wow, Robert, what is going on?" she asked, very confused.

Robert shook his head. He wasn't in the mood to start another battle. "Everything is alright. He just doesn't agree with a decision I made, but it is what is right for me. He will understand it when he has time to think about it."

A bit confused, she asked "What decision, Robert?"

He turned away from her, because he knew she was not likely to be supportive either. "I have signed up for the military, Sister. I report for duty next week." He waited for a response, but she was silent for quite a while.

After a long pause, she finally asked almost in a whisper, "You joined the military, and you are leaving? Why? Why on earth would you do such a thing?"

He turned toward her and lifted her hand in his. "Look, it is great opportunity for me. I could really use an adventure right now. And besides, they will give me medical training while I serve, so that I can come back and help take care of the town."

"I thought you were going to take over Father's congregation?" She was still confused.

"That was the plan, but I have been thinking an awful lot lately, and well...things have changed. Please, Sarah, I can't fight with you about it too. I really need your support on this. I know in my heart that this is the right move for me now." He turned his head slightly and gave her the sad face that always made her give in when they were younger.

She hated the sad face, because it did always make her laugh and eventually give into him. "I want to support you, but I hate this. You can't leave. We need you here. And Dad, what about him? Everything about the army goes against his beliefs. I don't know how he could ever accept this decision."

Robert reached out and pulled his sister to him. He hugged her tightly and whispered into her ear, "I know, that's why I need your help."

Sarah and her boys were devastated when Robert left. She managed to hold back her tears as he mounted his horse and they watched him ride off across the horizon, headed for Philadelphia. She was trying to be strong for her father's sake but lost her battle at bedtime and cried the entire night. Over the next few months, she worried about her father's health as each week he seemed to grow quieter and less active. His sermons had lost their energy and creativity, and many of the parishioners inquired about the pastor's health.

When the baby arrived, Sarah was unable to make the trip to visit and invited her father to stay with her for a while. He wanted to accept but did not feel that it would be appropriate to leave his church, so he declined. Sarah sent Ira to visit with him as often as she could and wrote him letters to send along. Ira tried to make her reports as positive as she could for Sarah, but both women knew that he was being consumed by his loneliness. Sarah was growing weak herself, trying to care for three young children, tend to the house, and worry about her father. She turned to Ivan for help. She explained her concerns to her husband and asked for his suggestions to help her father. Perhaps they could move back to the town so she could spend more time with him, or they could hire a full-time attendant to look after him. Ivan was uninterested in assisting anyone but himself, and that included Sarah's family. He did not understand why she would bring this to him—after all, he barely looked after his own family. She was disappointed but not surprised, so she continued to do the best she could for her father by sending letters, having her staff check up on him, and visiting when she could. When the baby was old enough to travel, she resumed her weekly visits, but her worries were not lessened, as it seemed to her that her father aged more each week. It was only a few more years until he passed.

Ivan gave her money to bury her father but could not be bothered to help her make the arrangements, or to attend the funeral. Sarah and the boys stayed in town for the entire week. Ira assisted through the final preparations and took care of the boys for Sarah. She wanted to suggest to her friend that she and the boys should stay in town and not return to Ivan's home but knew that she would be stepping way outside her boundaries to do so. She did not want to lose her job, or her friend. Everyone knew that Ivan was a horribly selfish man.

Her father's service was lovely, and Sarah very much appreciated the care and concern of the townsfolk that she had known all her life. Despite the grievous circumstances, she enjoyed visiting with them. The week went by very quickly, and the time to return home had come too soon. Before they began the journey home, she asked Ira to keep an eye on the boys so she could visit her father's grave one more time. As she sat in front of the marker, she dusted it with her palm. *If it is this dusty already, how dirty will it be in a month?* she wondered. Then tears began to stream down her face, knowing that she lived too far away to come and visit enough to take good care of the marker. She turned her head slightly to wipe the tear away with the back of her hand and noticed the silhouette of a man standing on the horizon. The sun was behind him, so she could only make out the outline of the figure. She knew that he was wearing a hat and long jacket but could not see his face. She called out to him, but he did not answer. He began to walk toward her. She wiped both her cheeks again and stood up to pull herself together. She squinted to try and make out the man's face but still could not. He continued to walk toward her. She wiped her dirty, wet hands on her skirt and called out to the man again. Again, he did not answer, but by now she could tell that the long jacket was a military uniform, and then she knew that the stranger was Robert. She began to cry hysterically. Her knees became weak, and she grabbed him hard without saying a word. She hugged him tightly and sobbed. She did not know if she was crying tears of joy or tears of sadness; she just knew that it felt pretty darn good to have her brother back, and she really needed to cry for a while.

Ivan started spending more and more time away from home. When he wasn't at work with his father, he was at the saloon with his brothers and friends. The more whiskey they drank, the more violent the stories became, and the more convinced the men became that someone needed to do something to protect the town from the tribes of natives that could attack at any moment. There was no evidence to suggest that an attack was imminent, but they were convinced that the stories had to be true. They began to take arms and patrol the acres on the outside of town, looking for evidence that trouble was approaching. Quite often, Ivan would be gone for days at a time, helping to protect the town from the threat he believed would be coming any day. Sarah did not really mind his absences too terribly much. She had never really developed a close relationship with her husband. She did what she had to do to keep the marriage civil but, other than their children, she and Ivan really had nothing in common. They did not dislike each other or resent the arrangement of their marriage. They simply were content to spend their time separately pursuing their own interests. She took care of the house and spent her time with her boys. She enjoyed sewing very much. She made all the clothing that her children wore and created dresses to donate to local families who needed help. She missed her father and their

Sunday visits very much, but Robert came to visit her from time to time.

Ivan and some of his drunken friends were camping one cold evening, about fifty miles south of town. They were in the process of herding a group of horses back to town that they had purchased in Virginia. On the last leg of their journey, they were exhausted and cranky. Quite frankly, the men were experiencing the frustration of spending way too much time together and were ready to fight over any little thing that upset them. They spent the entire day arguing and picking at one another, and now that they were drinking, the tension was getting worse. When an argument broke out between Ivan's brother John and Frank Barnes, John threw his whiskey bottle at the other man, smashing it on the ground right in front of him.

Ivan jumped up to separate the men before the situation came to physical blows. “Calm down, fellas,” he commanded. But the two continued to come at each other aggressively. Ivan turned his body to face John and pushed him back a step, away from the other man. “Come on, John, no fighting tonight.”

John looked down at his little brother. “Get out of the way, Ivan.”

Ivan became even more stern. “Not tonight, John. We are all too tired for this shit. Take a walk and walk it off.”

John glared for a few moments as more of the men began to stand up, prepared to break up the fight if it started. John made a huffing sound, spun around sharply, and stomped off into the forest. Everyone else relaxed back onto their makeshift seats around the fire and continued to pass the whiskey. John decided to check on the herd and walked out among the animals, checking each one to ensure that they were securely tethered for the night. He was quietly mumbling his complaints under his breath, rehashing all the things that he wished he would have said to old Frank Barnes during their argument. He knew his brother was right; even he was too tired for a fight tonight. As he moved past the last horse, a flicker of light far off in the distance caught his eye. *Someone else is camping down there,* he thought. He went back to the camp to gather a few guys to go with him and check this out.

The men gathered up all the weapons that they could carry, quickly drank as much alcohol as it took to make them feel brave, and hiked out across the plains toward the other campsite. The drunken marauders stumbled upon a small group of native elders from the Tuscarora tribe, who made their home many miles to the south. The twelve old men were traveling through the area, heading north to meet with other Iroquois elders in the fall. They had stopped to make camp along the river for the night and were all fast asleep when the drunken group discovered them. These men were not warriors, they were the politicians of the clan. They carried very few weapons to defend themselves and certainly were not planning to attack anyone.

Ivan's group intended to capture these men and take them back to town as their prisoners. As they entered the camp, the fire crackled and scared one of the larger marauders. He tripped backwards, falling onto one of the small tents that housed the sleeping elders. This woke the men and frightened them as well. They began to yell, and the drunken men yelled back. No one could understand the others' language, and chaos erupted. Everyone was scared and reacting to adrenaline. It was very dark, with only flashes of firelight. It did not take long until one of the drunkards panicked and hit the man in front of him, killing him instantly. This made the mob erupt into violence, and soon all twelve of the elders were dead.

The men stood in shock, covered in blood and disgusted with themselves. Killing these natives was nothing like they thought it would be. This was not like the stories they were told. There was no glory in this. It felt dirty and wrong. No one had intended to participate in such an act. They all wanted to run away but were afraid of the others in the group. Several men got sick, and one began to cry. They did not speak as they returned to the safety of their own camp. The trip home was eerily silent as well. Once back in their own warm homes, they did not tell anyone else about the awful thing that they had done.

None of the men returned to the tavern for the next few nights, except for Ivan. He was there on his usual stool, drinking his fill, eager to hear more stories about those who battled the savages from the west. But even he did not speak of the events from that night in the woods. Ivan and his brother John continued to drink heavily and continued to disappear night after night, trudging through the countryside, looking for the native attack they were so sure was coming to town. Their father became angrier by the day that his hung-over sons were falling behind with their farm work. He constantly pushed the boys to be more responsible and stay home with their families at night. They simply weren't interested.

Ivan and John headed out on another camping trip to once again scout the area for attacking natives. They loaded up the wagon and headed out into the forest north of town. For several days, they drank all night and spent the days wandering around the mountain, randomly shooting animals and trees. During another evening of extremely heavy drinking, the brothers decided to have a competition and see who could climb the highest on the rock face near camp. They staggered to the base and without any ropes or equipment began to climb as fast as they could. As they moved up the rock wall, they taunted one another and tried to nudge the other off balance. Higher and higher they climbed, cursing, laughing, each desperately trying to beat his brother to the top. John reached the peak first and pulled himself up over the edge to rest on the top. He laid flat on his back for a moment, trying to catch his breath. Then he leaned over the edge to make fun of the brother he had beaten. When he looked down, he was shocked. His brother was not there. He called out, with no response. *Where could he have gone? He should have been right behind me,* he thought. He called out again. "Ivan, where are you? Ivan!"

Then he realized what had happened. He looked to the bottom of the wall, and there was his brother's lifeless body lying twisted at the bottom. His brother had fallen to his death. He quickly climbed back down and tried to help Ivan, but it was too late. The alcohol and grief overcame him as he passed out in the dirt next to his dead brother.

As the sun rose in the morning, John woke up sober to what had happened. His father was going to be furious with him. He'd warned the boys to stop going out looking for trouble, he'd demanded that they stop their drinking and be more responsible around the farm. They did not follow his orders, and now his brother was dead. His father had been right, and he would not forgive John for this. He simply could not tell his family this horrible story. He was desperate. He sat and thought about his situation for a few hours, and finally decided to lie. He decided that he was going to blame his brother's death on the natives. He would claim that they were viciously attacked, and he was barely able to survive. Surely his father couldn't blame him if they were attacked and the red-skinned people killed his brother. He took his brother's gun and shot up the wagon. He tore his clothing and threw his supplies into the woods, as if they had been stolen. Finally, he took his hunting knife and stabbed his brother's body. He cried uncontrollably. *What kind of man can do this to his own brother?* he asked himself over and over. He had to continually drink from his whiskey bottle in order to find the strength to finish the job. He wrapped Ivan's body in the wagon tarp, cut himself in several places with the knife, and headed home to their father. *Hopefully, he will be grateful that I survived the attack and not angry at me that I killed his son.*

The charade worked on John's father. He believed that the natives had killed his boy, and for the first time since coming to this new world, believed that these people were indeed savages. He vowed vengeance on every tribe in the region. He poured every penny he could into assembling an army to crush the nearby villages, so that no one would ever lose an innocent son to these savages again. John kept quiet and let his father's fury continue to build and his rage continue to destroy.

After Ivan's funeral, home life became very tense for Sarah and her children. Ivan's father became angrier and angrier at the loss of his son. He was becoming consumed with the idea of getting revenge on the natives that he believed killed his youngest child. He gathered as many rough riders as he could find and armed them to hunt down the natives and keep his town safe. These drunken cowboys were creating tension and violence throughout the entire region.

Sarah took the boys to visit Robert as often as possible, so they would be away from the hatred that was building in the house. Ivan's family continued to support Sarah and her children, but with Ivan gone, she really did not feel like she belonged in the house. She never spoke to Robert about the awkwardness she felt at home, but he knew. He was concerned with the boys being exposed to the growing violence and tension.

Several families from town were moving north into the mountains to expand their logging businesses. They already had several cabins built and wanted Robert to join their new town, because of his military medical training. He spent months trying to convince Sarah to bring the boys and make the move with him. A fresh start would be good for them, and she could help start a school in the new town. She wanted to go, but moving her children away from the only home they had ever known was extremely intimidating to her. Robert continued to ply her with stories of new possibilities, and Ivan's father continued to scare her with his growing army of vigilantes. Finally, when the spring thaw rolled around once more, she packed up a wagon and took the boys with Robert up north.

Although the journey was not all that far, it took six days to complete. The wagons moved slow through the trees and bumpy terrain. Each night, Sarah lay under the stars, hugging her three boys tightly and wondering if she had made the right decision. She was scared, but Robert took care to reassure her as best he could. They were almost to the new town, and once she had a home of her own, he knew she would be happy. Robert was right. Late in the afternoon of the seventh day, the wagons finally made it to the top of the hill and into a large clearing. There were several small houses that formed an arch around the edge of the forest. At the top of the arch, there was another small building being constructed that was planned to be the town school. In the center of the clearing was a large willow tree with a small wooden sign etched with the name Willow Springs. Robert put his arm around his sister and squeezed her tightly. "Welcome to Willow

Springs, Sarah." He leaned over and kissed the top of her head. "Welcome home."

Sarah and her boys moved into a small cabin at the edge of the woods. It was a very small cabin that had only two rooms and a basement, but none of the boys seemed to mind. They helped their mother fix it up and make it into a warm, cozy home. They had not brought much with them but were able to use the resources around them to build what they needed. Robert built bunks for each of the boys in the loft, and Sarah planted a garden in the back yard. Her fears quickly dissolved as she busied herself building a new life for her children. Almost every week, more neighbors arrived in the small town and soon enough they were able to build a school, a church, and a small general store.

Sarah and her children were very happy in their new home. They quickly made friends, and the entire town became very close. She enjoyed once again being able to see her brother each day and greatly appreciated the strong male influence he had on her sons. Their father had never spent much time with them and his father certainly was not the type of influence that she wanted for her boys. Living in this new town was a great deal of hard work each day, but at night they all slept well. They were together, they were safe, and they were surrounded with good, caring people.

CHAPTER FIVE

EVERYONE WHO ARRIVED IN THE NEW LITTLE TOWN seemed to bring more skills and supplies to help the community develop. Whatever they didn't have, they found a way to make or do without. The next closest town was several days away by horseback. They were secluded in the mountains, but that was exactly the way they wanted it. Life was simple and challenging. They had few luxuries, but the town was growing and the view was breathtaking. The townsfolk learned from each other and took care of each other.

It was only a few months into their new life that Robert brought the boys some news that they found greatly disappointing. "The school is completed and ready, kids. And the new teacher is scheduled to arrive next week."

"Aww," they all three grumbled.

Laughing, Robert patted his youngest nephew, Elliot, on top of his curly-haired head. "What are you griping about, little one? You aren't even old enough to go to school yet."

Sarah laughed as well. Secretly, she was looking forward to the school opening and having the boys out of the house for a few hours each day, but she decided to play along with the boys. "Oh darn, you poor guys will have to go back to school. That's awful. I will miss you so much." She couldn't keep a straight face and started laughing out loud again. The boys didn't appreciate her attempt to be funny and went off to play.

Over the next few days, Sarah worked on helping the other mothers trade clothing and stitch new items to make sure that all the children had something to wear to school. The new teacher arrived on schedule, and they all helped her settle into her new home next to the school. A few days later, all the children reported for duty, and school was in session. Life in Willow Springs was becoming conventional.

One evening, Sarah left her boys at the table to work on their studies and headed down to the basement to get a few things. No sooner had she reached the bottom stair than she heard their chairs bumping around and the kids running across the floor. *What is all that commotion?* she wondered. As she turned and headed back up the steps, she shook her head in disbelief. *It is simply amazing how fast those guys can go from calm and quiet to full-on rough housing.* As she got to the top of the stairs, she saw the three boys plastered up against the window, calling out for her.

She was startled by how much commotion three small boys could cause. "What in the good Lord's name is going on here?" she asked.

"Mama, Mama, there's a really big bear."

"Oh, there's a bear, is there?" She giggled, thinking that they were being silly, and looked out the window. By the time she got to the window, the bear had disappeared back into the wilderness, and she continued to laugh at her boys. When the boys' excitement didn't fade and they continued to insist that they saw a bear, she grabbed her gun and went out the back door to humor them and play along. As she opened the door to run outside, she almost tripped over Xuan's tiny body huddled on the porch.

"Oh my gracious!" she exclaimed. Sarah stood frozen for a moment. Then her motherly instincts kicked in, and she bent down to scoop the child up in her arms and ran inside. She placed her on the bed and swaddled her in blankets to keep her warm.

She turned to call out to her sons for help, but they were already right behind her.

"Elliot, get me a pail of water and some cloth. Jason, run quickly and fetch your uncle. Tell him to bring his medical bag. Isaac, come to Mama and help me get her warm."

She looked up at her boys, who were standing in shock, trying to figure out where their mother got a little dark-skinned girl.

"Move it, boys," she snapped. The boys began to hustle to their chores. Just as Jason got out the door, Sarah stopped him. "Jason" she yelled.

"Yes, ma'am?" he asked as his head popped back inside the door frame.

"Be careful, please," she pleaded.

Jason rolled his eyes at his mother's concern. After all, he was twelve years old now, almost a man.

When Elliot returned with the water, Sarah dipped a clean cloth into the bucket and allowed the water to drip onto Xuan's dry, cracked lips. The girl began to move a bit, and Sarah continued to try to get water into her. Then she cleaned the girl's wounds and applied antiseptic to ward off infection.

"Where did you come from, sweetheart?" she asked as she continued to attend to the girl.

Her youngest son Isaac leaned close to his mother and whispered, "I don't think she can hear you, Mama."

Sarah smiled and brushed the blonde curls out of his eyes. Isaac helped his mother clean and dress all the little girl's wounds. They took turns dripping water onto her lips, trying to get her to drink. Xuan began to shiver, and Isaac ran to his bunk to get his favorite blanket to tuck tightly around her shoulders.

Sarah's brother Robert pushed open the cabin door, calling out to her, "Sarah, Jason is telling me a wild story that you found a little girl..." He stopped in mid-sentence as he swung around the door and saw Sarah sitting on the edge of the bed. He stood confused for a moment, and then his medical training took over and he began feverishly working to save the little girl's life. When Robert had done all that he could for his tiny patient, he helped Sarah tuck the boys into bed, and then sat with his sister to keep a vigil throughout the night.

"Sarah," he asked, "where did she come from?"

"I am not sure. The boys heard a noise outside, they thought it was a bear." The two adults laughed, thinking the boys' imagination had gotten the best of them. "I opened the door to check the yard, and there she was, collapsed on the back porch. How close do you suppose the nearest tribe village is from here?" she asked her brother.

"I thought it was a great distance," he replied. "After all, the purpose of moving here was to be far away from the raiders who are murdering these people, and the retaliation that is sure to follow."

Just then, Xuan wiggled in her sleep and let out a moan. Robert went to check on her and then returned to his sister's side.

"Her village must have been attacked, but I am not sure how she survived. She is so thin and dehydrated. We need to get her to eat or drink something." He continued to keep a close eye on the girl as he spoke.

"She is so tiny, Robert. She can't be more than six or seven years old. How did she find us?"

He finally took his eyes off his patient and turned to look into his sister's eyes. "Sarah, you are such a loving woman," he said with a warm smile. "I can't say if it was our God or hers, but someone who is protecting this child brought her to you, because they knew she would be loved and well cared for in this house."

Sarah leaned forward and hugged her brother, then nestled her head on his shoulder and fell asleep. The adults took turns throughout the night waking to try to get Xuan to drink some water. Issac, who was about the same age as Xuan, immediately became infatuated with his tiny new friend. He woke before the sun's first light to check on her and helped his mother and uncle day after day to tend to her. He was very much delighted when she began to awaken for short periods of time.

Sarah collected some material to make the girl a clean dress. She was an accomplished seamstress and had considered created a beautiful, frilly dress for her, but decided that perhaps she would be more comfortable in a dress resembling the one she was wearing now. She was attempting to create a pair of shoes for her when Isaac asked for permission to share a pair of his.

After more than a week, Xuan had made it through the worst and appeared to be gaining some weight. She was not frightened by these white people. They were kind to her, and staying with them meant that she would not be alone in the wilderness any more.

Isaac adored his new little friend. When she had regained enough energy to run around and play, they were inseparable. He very much became her protector and took her everywhere he went. They took turns pointing to objects and teaching each other what their people called the item. Xuan learned the English words but rarely spoke any. She had little need to speak, as Isaac made sure she had everything she needed all the time. At night, she would snuggle tightly against Sarah and drift off to dream about her own mother. She missed her home terribly and would often weep in her sleep. Sarah's heart would break each night, knowing that there was little she could do to ease the girl's pain. Still, she sat up night after night to console her.

After a few weeks, Sarah decided to attempt to unravel the knotted mess of hair Xuan had, so she could wash it. She sent her boys to get pails of water, warmed them slightly on the fire and took them into the root cellar.

"Alright, little miss, you are coming with me," she said, smiling, to Xuan. She followed obediently, but as soon as Sarah began to sort through the tangles, she began to get upset. The woman tried to console her but was determined that she was going to complete the task, no matter how much the child protested. She was as gentle as possible and reassured Xuan constantly that the process would not hurt.

"Sweety, you will feel so much better with clean hair," she told her. And then she giggled a bit as she showed the little girl a twig that she'd pulled from the mess. Xuan put her hand on her hair as if she understood that the stick had been stuck in her hair. She still was not happy about having her hair touched, but she tried to sit still and cooperate. Sarah worked carefully with the wooden comb to untangle and separate each section of the girl's hair. Every few minutes, Xuan would cry out and try to pull away, but the determined woman held her and continued her mission and reassured her once again.

The boys were playing upstairs in the cabin, each one hoping they were not next in line for hair washing. Isaac was concerned for his friend when he heard her cries. He knew his mother would never hurt her, but it upset him to hear the whines. He peered down the stairs to the cellar a few times. He considered going down to console Xuan, but he hated to have his hair washed and could not risk giving his mom the idea that he wanted his done next.

As Xuan let out another yell, the boys heard a loud rumbling sound. The two older boys jumped up from the floor and yelled to Isaac, "What did you do?

Isaac ran to hide between his bigger brothers. "I didn't do it," he protested. Then they heard the rumbling again but this time it seemed to be closer to the cabin. The boys huddled close together and looked all around the room, trying to figure out what was happening.

Sarah did not hear the mysterious noise and continued to pick at her patient's hair. When she finally got most of the tangles straightened, she moved to the wooden trough, grabbed the soap bar and began to pour water onto Xuan's hair. She tried hard not to get any water into the little girl's eyes, but with her kicking and screaming, that was not easy. Xuan let out a loud shriek as the first wave of water washed over her head, which made the boys jump and turn in unison toward the cellar entrance.

The older boys quickly tried to act as if they had not been scared and laughed at Isaac for jumping. Before Isaac could argue back with them, they heard a long, deep growl that sounded like it was coming from directly outside the cabin door. They huddled together once again and called out to their mother, who could not hear them over Xuan's cries. Sarah continued to wash the girl's hair, and Xuan continued to cry louder and louder. The louder her cries became, the louder the growling outside the door became, and the more afraid the boys became. They finally split up and ran to the cracks in the cabin walls to peek out in all directions in an attempt to discover what monster was lurking outside their home.

The growls became louder and louder, and the walls began to shake. Whatever was outside was trying to break in. The boys cried out for their mother once again with no response. They ran to the center of the room and huddled closely under the table.

"It's going to break down the walls!" cried Jason. "What do we do?"

The thunderous growl was now deafening loud, and the boys shivered uncontrollably. Dishes fell from the shelves, pictures fell off the walls, and the boards that held the tiny cabin together were squeaking as if they were about to give in. The boys began to cry in fear and crouched together under the dining table.

Finally, Sarah had finished rinsing the soap from Xuan's locks. She gently rubbed a towel over her head to soak up the excess water, pulled a strand of the girl's hair up to her little nose and said, "Smell," and then she inhaled really hard herself to show Xuan what she meant. "Doesn't that smell nice?" she asked. The child stopped crying and smiled. Her hair did smell pretty, and she did feel better being clean. She was still mad at Sarah for making her get her hair washed, but she kept smelling her pretty hair.

As soon as Xuan's tears stopped, so did the attack upstairs. Just as the boys were convinced they were all going to be eaten by some mysterious monster, the house stopped shaking and grew eerily silent. They climbed out from under the table and carefully looked out the window to see nothing. They did not speak, they just looked at one another, very confused.

Then, all of a sudden, the silence was broken by a sound that once again scared the boys. Their mother was coming up out of the cellar. They knew she would never believe their story, and that they would get blamed for the mess. Without words, they quickly began picking up the dishes and hanging the pictures as Jason blocked the cellar entrance to stall their mother.

"Xuan, did you get your hair washed?" he asked as he bent down to talk to her and to block his mother's progress. Xuan did not understand what he was saying until he patted her on her head. She smiled back at him and lifted a lock of her hair to his nose.

"Ummmm," Jason laughed. "You smell pretty." She did not understand his words, but she did understand his smile.

"Jason, can we come up now?' Sarah asked.

Jason considered for a moment asking his mother to wash his hair in order to give his brothers more time to clean, but decided that he wasn't quite willing to make that much of a sacrifice. He stood up slowly and moved out of her way, waiting for her to yell. Luckily, she did not. She wiped the dust off the table with her hand and simply said, "I do wish you boys would not play so rough inside the house."

They just couldn't believe that she did not hear the loud, rumbling growls. It was the loudest commotion they had ever heard in their life, and their mother seemed oblivious to it. All through dinner that night, the boys continued to take turns peeking out the window to make sure the intruder was not returning to their porch.

As the days rolled on, the little native girl settled into her new family and tried her best to learn their strange ways. The boys took her everywhere they went. Sarah decided not to send Xuan to the local school until she understood the language better. So, every day the boys headed off to class, and the little girl sadly watched them leave. Sarah created games to teach Xuan at home.

Xuan was becoming quite a help around the house. She would watch Sarah as she did her daily chores and do what she could to assist. When Sarah did the mending for the neighbors, the little girl would sit very still and watch intently. She was sure she could do it also, but Sarah would not let her try.

"Sweetheart, you are too little," she would say lovingly. "The needles are too sharp."

Xuan waited anxiously every afternoon for the boys to return home from school. They would all go outside to do their chores together, and then play in the yard until darkness fell before returning to the cabin for dinner. After the dinner dishes were cleaned and put away, the boys would sit at the table for homework, and Xuan would sit with them and draw with Isaac's crayons. He was so proud to share everything he had with her. Many evenings, Uncle Robert would stop by to visit. They were such a happy family.

One evening after chores, the kids ran through the yard playing a game of hide-and-seek. Xuan ran as fast as she could and ducked behind the water well when it was her turn to hide. The boys could easily find her when they played, because she always hid in the same place and giggled loudly the entire time she was hiding, but they played along and pretended to be unable to find her. They always allowed her to win the game. This time her giggling was interrupted when she heard someone yelling at Elliot. She quietly slipped around the back of the barn to see what was going on. When she peeked around the corner, she saw three kids walking toward Elliot, and Jason giving them a hard time.

"Roger Webber, what are you doing here?" she heard Jason ask the largest kid.

"What's the matter, you little sissy, are you scared?" one of the other boys asked in a whiny voice.

Elliot tugged on Jason's arm. "Come on, Jason, let's go to the house."

Jason agreed with his little brother that they should turn and walk away from the confrontation and went to find Isaac and Xuan. Roger ran up behind him and pushed him with both hands, so hard that he stumbled and almost fell to the ground.

"Don't walk away from me, you little punk," he yelled at Jason. "I saw you on the swing today with Abigail. She is my girlfriend."

"What?" demanded Jason. "Abigail came and sat with me. Anyway, she would never go out with a bully like you."

Roger became furious at that point and swung his fist hard at Jason's face. Jason ducked out of the way at the last moment, put his hands on the bully's shoulders, and pushed him to the ground.

"Go away, Roger," he said as he turned and started walking to the house. Xuan came running from behind the barn to make sure her boys were alright. Roger was embarrassed in front of his best pals. He was fuming and wanted revenge for being embarrassed. He picked up a rock and hurled it as hard as he could at the back of Jason's head. Once again, he missed his target and the rock floated straight past Jason and hit Xuan on the side of her head. The impact knocked her to the ground. The rock was flat and grazed her ear, so it did not do any serious damage. It did scare her, and she began to scream like an angry six-year-old girl, which terrified the boys, and they ran away. Elliot quickly pulled Xuan to her feet, brushed the dirt out of her hair, and hugged her tightly until her shrieking turned to sobs. Then he took her inside to his mother to get checked out.

Sarah heard the crying and met them at the door to find out what had happened.

"Oh, that Roger Webber is such a nasty, nasty little boy," Sarah huffed as she put a cold, wet cloth on the side of Xuan's head. "I am going straight over to their house in the morning to give his mother a piece of my mind." Then she scooped Xuan into her arms and settled onto the rocker. She rubbed the little girl's head and sang to her until she fell asleep. After a while, she tucked her into bed and helped the boys with their homework.

Roger and his friends ran off as soon as they realized that he'd hit the little girl with the rock. Roger was a bully to his classmates but had no intention of hurting someone smaller than him. They ran down the tree line as fast as they could toward Roger's house, until it became hard to breathe.

One of the boys called out to Roger, "You know Jason is going to be angry with you tomorrow at class for hurting his sister."

"That is not his sister," Roger yelled back. "That little native brat doesn't belong in our town, her people are savages. My father says the town should get rid of her before she gets old enough to kill us all in our sleep. That's what her people do, you know? It's in her blood."

The other boys just looked at him. They had not heard the stories that Roger's father had about native raids on the white settlers. They simply could not see Xuan as anything but a tiny, helpless little girl.

The boy shook his head and laughed at Roger. "Whatever, Roger, you just better watch out for Jason."

The boys walked for a few more minutes when they realized how quickly night was setting in.

"Wow, it sure is getting dark fast tonight," one of the boys commented. "Wait, did you hear that?" he asked as he moved closer the other two boys.

"Hear what, you big chicken?" snarled Roger.

"I was sure I heard a growl coming from those trees over there. It sounded pretty big."

"You are crazy. Keep walking," Roger demanded as he started walking quickly. The other two boys stopped for a moment and stood together, looking around. They were afraid to move toward the trees.

Then another growl filled the air, loud enough this time for all the boys to hear. Roger spun around to look where his friends were. All three boys stood silently for a moment. They heard another growl, but this time it sounded as if it came from the other side of the path. Confused, the boys listened intently to try and determine what they were dealing with and where exactly it was coming from.

Another long growl, this time it sounded like it was right on top of them. They spun around expecting to see an animal, but all they saw was darkness. All three boys, including big, tough Roger, were shaking in fear.

A dark fog started to manifest just behind Roger and seemed to be moving toward him, growing bigger the closer it became. The boys wanted desperately to warn their friend, but fear had stolen their voices. The older boy managed to lift his shaking hand and point behind Roger as the mist seemed to be right behind him.

"What?" Roger asked in a somewhat whiny voice. He saw the color drain from his friends' faces and was absolutely terrified. He began to run toward his friends, but then curiosity struck and he just had to see what he was running from. He stopped running and slowly turned around to look. Just as he did, the dark fog spread upward in the shape of a giant bear and fell on top of him, encasing his entire body. The boys could not see their friend inside the monstrous cloud. They started toward him, thinking they could pull him out of it, but when they got close, it wisped up high into the air and disappeared into the dark forest, taking Roger with it.

The boys stood in shock for a moment, and then finally found their voices. "Roger," they yelled in unison as they began to run into the woods to find their friend. Another growl—this time it was so deafening, they thought that it might be thunder. The growl went on for what seemed like minutes, and the boys felt a hot breath on their faces, as if the beast were standing right in front of them.

Without words, they both made the decision to abandon their friend and try to save themselves. They ran screaming to their homes. They had totally succumbed to their fear. They could no longer think, they could only run and scream. Their hearts were beating so heavily that their vision grew dark, and they struggled to get air into their lungs. When they arrived in the safety of their parents' care, both boys chose to forsake their friend and not tell their story. They retired to their beds, hoping to find Roger sitting in class the next morning when they arrived at school.

When the sun came up, Sarah got the boys off to school and cleaned up the breakfast dishes. She brushed Xuan's hair back to check her head where the rock had hit her. The swelling had subsided, and there was barely a mark, but Sarah was still angry. She wrapped the tiny shawl that she had crocheted around Xuan's shoulders and grabbed her own, and then headed out the door toward Roger's house. Just as she crossed the porch, she saw her boys running back to the house.

"Ma, we have the day off school today," Jason called out excitedly. "Teacher sent us home."

"Why on earth would she do that? Did you get in trouble?"

"No, Mama, everyone got sent home so the adults can go look for Roger." Elliot pushed past his mother and took Xuan in the house to play.

Confused, Sarah looked to her older boys for an explanation. "Look for Roger? Would that be Roger Webber?"

Jason looked upset, so Isaac answered the question. "Yeah, Miss Keller said he never went home last night. No one knows where he is, so they are searching the woods. They think a wild animal got him." Jason's gaze sank to the ground with guilt. He had nothing to do with the disappearance, but it did not feel right to him to have had a fight with him just before something bad happened to him.

Sarah grabbed the two boys and pulled them close in a hug. "That is awful," she whispered. "I am so glad you boys are safe. I don't know what I would do if anything ever happened to my boys."

They hugged for a moment, and then Isaac pulled back a bit and said, "And now your little girl."

Sarah smiled and agreed. *And now my little girl,* she thought.

Sarah enjoyed having the kids home that day, even if it was under such unfortunate circumstances. They played in the yard most of the day, and then did chores in the evening. Uncle Robert stopped by that night after the boys had gone to bed and shared the sad news that even though the townsfolk had searched for miles, there was no sign of poor Roger. The townspeople continued to search for weeks for the boy but never discovered any clue to finding him. His friends remained silent, fearing that no one would believe them if they shared what they had seen. Roger's parents eventually gave up hope and erected a stone in the local cemetery.

As time went by, the small village of Willow Springs grew into a lovely town. Each year a few more families chose to settle down there, and the townspeople would chip in to build them a cabin to live in. Each new family brought a skill set that would aid the town's survival. There were several farmers, hunters, a blacksmith, carpenters, and the doctor. When the Fergusons arrived, they opened the town's general store and arranged for supplies to be delivered to town once a week. Eventually when the mail service began in the area, the supply truck would bring the town's mail to them as well. As the population spread out across the mountain, they were always careful to keep the church in the center of village.

Isaac and Xuan were the very best of friends. They shared everything, and each afternoon, as soon as the final bell rang at school, Isaac burst out of the schoolhouse and ran all the way home to tell his friend about his day. Before long the entire town noticed that Xuan was not growing. At first Sarah did not think much of it, as she continuously had to make bigger clothing for the boys, but the little girl's dress size remained the same. After all, boys do grow much faster than girls sometimes. But as the years went by, she became concerned. Robert checked Xuan and did all the tests that he had access to in the tiny town but found nothing medically wrong with the little girl. Jason, Elliot, and Isaac were growing into adulthood, but tiny Xuan was still the size of a six-year-old.

Sarah knew that someday soon her boys would meet their wives and would go off and start their own families. Part of her really liked the idea of permanently having a little one in the house with her. But as time went by, and the years began to take a toll on Sarah's body, she worried about who would care for her little red-skinned princess when she passed on.

Robert helped her to bind parchment pages between two thick pieces of tree bark. Inside they documented stories and created pictures telling all they knew of the story of Xuan, and how to care for her. The night before Isaac's wedding, she left Xuan with Robert, wrapped the book in a blanket, and took it to visit Isaac's bride, Rebecca.

Rebecca had known the family for many years and was shocked that she'd never realized Xuan had been a little girl the entire time. After gently flipping through the pages, she sat silent for moment. She knew it was true that the girl was not aging, but she was trying to figure out how this could even be possible.

“I can't believe it never occurred to me that she has always been a little girl,” Rebecca finally said.

Sarah leaned forward and gently clasped Rebecca's hand inside both of her own.

“I know this a lot to ask the day before your wedding, but I am worried about what will happen to her when I pass. I mean, who will take care of this special little girl?”

Rebecca smiled to reassure her soon to be mother-in-law.

“Please don't worry, Miss Sarah,” she said lovingly. “Isaac absolutely adores Xuan. He has already spoken about having her and you both live with us, once we get settled. We will always be there for you both.”

And so it went for the little native princess. She became the Ingram family heirloom, so to speak. Just as the land and homes of the town of Willow Springs, Pennsylvania, were passed down from generation to generation, little Xuan was passed through the generations of the Ingram family. She would watch their children be born, play with them as children, and then they would care for her when they were ready to have their own children. Time after time she would stand by their graves as they passed and returned to the earth. Each generation added to the stories and pictures in Xuan's journal.

Every family in the small, secluded town cherished their little secret and protected her from the outside world, which was not difficult to do, since they very rarely received visitors. Willow Spring's only access road runs out of the city of Wilkes-Barre, and is twenty miles long. The road was a dirt horse trail until the 1940s, when the state put down a coat of macadam over it. It has barely been maintained since then, which is how the townspeople like it. The only vehicles that travel the beat-up back road are family members of the current residents, and the delivery truck that still brings their mail and supplies for Ferguson's General Store and Maisey's Hometown Diner every Wednesday afternoon. Occasionally over the years, some real estate developers have visited the town, trying to convince the folks to give up their homes. The view from the top of their mountain is spectacular, and when autumn comes and the leaves turn color, it becomes even more breathtaking. Because many tourists travel to the area to tour the foliage and take pictures, developers view it as a prime spot for a vacation resort. Not to mention that the back side of the mountain is filled with hot springs that they could market as "therapeutic" to make more of a profit. None of the families in town were ever interested in selling their homes, and they continued to be passed down generation after generation.

CHAPTER SIX

Current-day Lancaster, Pennsylvania

THE PHONE BLARED THROUGH the small city apartment in the early hours of the morning. Benjamin had just crashed on the bed after a twenty-hour shift in the Lancaster Memorial Hospital's emergency room. He was severely exhausted, but the phone rang insensately, and finally he had to give in and answer it.

"Hello," he muttered into the handset before he realized he was holding it upside-down. As he flipped it around, he could hear a man's voice speaking on the other end.

"Hello, hello," the voice repeated. "Is this Benjamin Bashore, Dr. Benjamin Bashore?"

"Yeah, speaking." He did not recognize the voice and could not seem to wake himself enough to comprehend what was going on.

"Dr. Bashore, was your father Harold Bashore, and your mother named Ann Marie?"

Ben sat up and became concerned who could possibly be asking about his parents. They both had passed away quite a while ago.

"Yes, those were my parents' names. Who is this, and what do you want?" he demanded.

"Dr. Bashore, I am afraid I have some rather sad news for you. My name is Thomas Lincoln. I am the attorney for your uncle, Leonard Bashore." There was a pause. "Dr. Bashore, I am terribly sorry to tell you this, but your uncle has passed away."

Ben stood up and ran his hand up across his forehead to push the hair out of his eyes. "What, my uncle has passed? How did he die? When is the funeral?"

"Dr. Bashore, I am terribly sorry. Your uncle's affairs were not incredibly organized, and it took me a while to locate you," the attorney apologized. "The funeral was last week. I am so very sorry."

"Oh," he said as he sank back down onto the bed. "Well then, is there anything that I need to take care of?" He didn't really know much about his uncle or what family there was left.

"Yes sir, that is exactly why I am reaching out to you today. As the only living relative, your uncle's official will is said to apportion his entire estate to you," the man on the phone informed him.

Ben suspected that he was the last surviving member of the Bashore family, but it was very depressing to hear it said out loud. Still groggy from his exhausting shift, the conversation was sinking in very slowly. "His estate, you say? What exactly are we talking about here?"

"Your uncle had a home and several acres of land in Willow Springs, Pennsylvania. The property, the house, and everything inside it now belongs to you. There were no bank accounts, as Leonard did not believe in the banking system. His funeral and burial plot were prepaid, so there are no expenses that you are responsible for." There was a long pause as the attorney flipped through more pages of the will to ensure that he'd covered everything he needed to. "And as you are aware, I am sure, your uncle was still practicing medicine right up until the end, so you inherit his office, equipment, and patients as well, if you would like to take over the business."

"Wow, I would have thought Uncle Leonard would have retired by now," Benjamin said while trying to figure out in his head how old his uncle would have been by now.

"No sir, he was the only doctor in the town. The good people of Willow Springs are in need of a new doctor to take care of them now that Dr. Bashore is gone. They like to keep things in the family, you know. Been that way for many generations."

Ben chuckled a bit. "I'm not sure I am ready for my own practice just yet. Do I need to sign some papers or something for you? What should I do next?"

"I will need you to come by my office at your convenience to transfer the estate to your name and file some paperwork with the state. I can give you my number, and you can call me to schedule an appointment when you are ready. And once again, Benjamin, I am very sorry that I did not find you in time for the funeral."

The doctor wasn't exactly sure where his uncle had lived. He'd visited there a few times when he was a small boy but could not quite remember how far of a trip it would be to go see the house that was left to him. He also had to speak with his fiancée, Diana, before making plans for a trip. He wrote down the attorney's name and number, and then climbed back into bed for some much-needed slumber.

When he finally woke a few hours later, it was time to head back to the hospital. Ben was working so many hours and barely had time to think, so a few days had passed before he had a chance to discuss the matter of his uncle's estate with Diana. She surprised him late one night by popping into the emergency ward while he was working.

“Hey, sexy medicine man, how much longer is it until you can take a break?” she joked as she jumped in front of him.

He smiled and kissed her on her forehead. “Hey baby, what are doing here?”

“I miss you and thought maybe you could sneak out for a little while, and we could grab a cup of coffee.” She could see that he wasn't crazy about leaving his duties, so she kept moving in front of him while he attempted to work.

He finally gave in. “Alright, I will meet you in the cafeteria in ten minutes.”

She giggled and shook her head. “Dr. Bashore, you are a workaholic. You feel guilty about taking a little break, while everyone else around here has no problem disappearing for hours.”

He put his hand gently over her lips so none of his coworkers would hear her. “Ten minutes, I promise.” He leaned down to sneak in another quick kiss, and then ducked into an exam room and slid the curtain shut. It did not take him long to tend to his patient, and when he was finished, he joined his lovely lady in the cafeteria for an awful cup of coffee.

It was a nice visit, and he always wished that he had more time to spend with her. He was happy that she'd stopped by to surprise him, but he did wonder about her motives.

“You received a letter in the mail today from an attorney upstate,” she explained as she pulled the envelope from her bag. “Is everything alright?”

He smiled to reassure her and put his hand on top of hers. He told her the story about his uncle's passing. They spoke about his family history and how there really was no one left now. He opened the letter, which recapped the conversation he'd had on the phone. He slid the letter over to Diana to read, and then they began to work out the details of how and when they would be able to visit the attorney and take care of all the necessary paperwork. Their schedules were both so crazy, it seemed impossible to them that they would be able to take time out to visit the house, let alone handle the task of cleaning it out and selling it.

"Let's just do it," Diana finally suggested. "We are both so exhausted, let's take two weeks off, drive up and sign the papers, and then visit Willow Springs. We can stay in the house and get our thoughts organized. It would be a little free vacation, and Lord knows we both could use a vacation." He knew that somehow he was going to have to make the time to deal with the estate, but there were a hundred and ten reasons why it just wasn't the right time to take time off work. But the more they discussed it, the more he realized that the house would probably rot into dust before there ever was a right time to take time off from the hospital. So, he agreed to rearrange his schedule and make it happen. Diana was excited that he'd finally agreed and spent the entire next day planning their trip. It certainly wasn't the vacation she was dreaming of, but if it got her man away from the stress of the hospital for a few days, she would take it happily. They worked out all the details and were ready to leave the following Monday.

Diana was bustling with excitement as they loaded the car for the trip. It had been months since they were able to even take a day off together, let alone take an actual vacation. She did not know much about Ben's childhood, since his parents had passed before she met him and he did not have any siblings. She was hoping that visiting his uncle's house would encourage him to share more details about his life before they met.

After she loaded her SUV with absolutely everything she thought that they could possibly need during the next two weeks, she went back into the apartment to pack a picnic lunch for the way up. Ben had taken their Saint Bernard to the kennel for safekeeping during their time away. She was all ready to go and just had to wait for his return. She sat on the stoop, drinking her cup of coffee and waiting for him to get back from the kennel.

She jumped up when she saw his pickup pull up to the curb and was excited to finally be getting underway. Ben was not happy when he slid out of the driver's seat and slammed the truck door.

"I am afraid we have a small problem." he said as he gripped the handle to the rear truck door. "Well, actually a very large, slobbering problem." He slid the door open, and their giant dog jumped out. He was excited from his ride and jumped up at Diana, almost knocking her to the ground.

"What? Why is he here, what happened to the kennel?" she asked, trying to maintain her footing and laughing at the dog. "Barley, take it easy."

"Problem at the kennel, they can't keep him. I guess I will call the attorney and reschedule the appointment." Ben headed into the apartment to make the call.

Diana had been trying for months to get this guy to take a few days off work to go somewhere, anywhere other than the hospital or apartment. She was not about to give up her vacation plans quite so easily.

"No, Ben," she yelled at him and spun around to stop his progress toward the door. "We will take him with us.

"Take him with us?" Ben looked at her as if she were crazy. "Take our giant dog on a four-hour drive?"

"Yeah, he loves to be outside, and it's not like we are staying in a hotel. He will like it, I am sure. He can play outside and romp through the forest."

"But he is big, and hairy, and did you smell his breath lately?" Ben was getting a little whiny. "Do you really want to be in a car with him for that long of a time? It's hot, and he is going to pest."

Diana tilted her head to the side and smiled like she did when one of her kindergarten students whined to her. "Ben, you are not getting out of this trip for any reason, so it looks like he is coming. Accept it and put him in the car."

He handed her the dog's leash. "Alright, you win. You put him in the car, and I will pack some of his stuff to take with us." He trotted back into the apartment like a disagreeable toddler.

Diana giggled. Her soon-to-be husband reminded her of one of her students. *That's right, never mess with a teacher*, she thought to herself, and then turned to the energetic dog. "Come on Barley, you and Mommy are going bye-bye."

A little while later, they had Barley all packed up and ready for the four-hour drive to the Wilkes-Barre court house to meet the attorney.

The drive up through the eastern side of Pennsylvania is very scenic, with rolling hills filled with trees as far as the eye can see. The sky was bright blue with huge white, puffy clouds. It was strikingly beautiful with the sun bouncing off the top of them. They looked for cloud formations that were shaped liked animals for a while on the drive. Diana admired the amazing rock formations along the highway, and Barley ran from side to side across the back seat to bark at the birds that flew overhead. At one point, Diana thought that the dog was going to jump out the window when he spotted a small heard of white-tailed deer grazing along the road.

"Is he ever going to lay down and take a nap?" Ben grumbled. Diana giggled and put her hand on Ben's leg.

"Probably not."

After several hours on the road, they decided to stop at a travel rest stop to take Barley for a short walk. Ben grabbed the leash. "Let me walk him. He is so wound up right now that I am afraid he will run away and pull you off into the woods." He leaned forward and kissed her cheek as he took the dog from her. Barley was very difficult to hold onto. He ran straight for the trees and dug through the ground cover, looking for insects and small animals. A chipmunk caught his eye, almost as if it were teasing him, and he bolted out after it. It snickered and ran higher into the tree. Ben pulled on the leash with both hands, trying to encourage the dog to head back to the car. After about forty-five minutes, they were finally able to get back onto the road and continue up Route 81 past all the little towns that led them to their destination, much like the numbers on a connect-the-dot puzzle.

When they finally arrived in the city of Wilkes-Barre, they navigated their way through the streets, twisting and turning until they eventually found the courthouse. They were actually a bit ahead of schedule to meet the attorney, so they left Barley in the car and got out to stretch their legs. The courthouse was a gigantic square building with intricate architecture on each side. It was a beautiful building, with artwork skillfully planned to catch your eye from every angle. It sits by itself in the center of a city block, surrounded by lawn and immaculate landscaping. Ben and Diana walked completely around the entire building in awe, admiring the architecture. They imagined that the building must be very old. As they rounded the back of the building, Diana noticed a path that led down to the Susquehanna River, which runs through the center of the city.

"Oh look, Ben, they have a river walk."

Ben was confused why this was interesting to her and waited for more information.

"While you are meeting with the lawyer, I will take Barley for a walk along the river."

And so, that was the plan. Ben nervously gathered up his paperwork from the car and headed up the long cement staircase that led up the front of the courthouse, while Diana wrestled with the giant, hairy dog to get him out of the car and down to the path. He paused for a moment when he reached the top of the stairs to watch Barley drag her across the lawn. She pulled back on the leash as hard as she could, but the dog was excited to explore every bush and tree. *This is such a bad idea,* he worried to himself. *I am going to come out of here and find out that the darn dog knocked someone's child into the river or ate somebody's poodle.* Diana looked up at him with a warm, loving smile. She waved and then gave him a thumbs-up of encouragement. Ben faked a smile and waved back, then turned and went inside.

Once inside, he made his way through the metal detectors and into the lobby. He stopped once again to admire the design of the great building. It was like walking into a Roman temple. The walls were adorned with carvings of the Lady Justice and other robed figures. In the center of the shiny tile floor was the city crest etched into marble. It was very impressive. He wished he had more time to visit this city and explore more of the architecture and history, but there was too much to do at his uncle's house. He walked forward to the elevators and studied the directory to find his attorney's office. When he arrived at the office, he waited nervously in the reception room for what seemed like a very long period of time. Finally, Mr. Lincoln came out of his office and greeted Ben with a handshake.

"Dr. Bashore, I apologize for keeping you waiting." The lawyer shook Ben's hand, and then motioned for him to enter the office and take a seat. "How was your drive up north?"

Ben slid down into a thick leather chair and was pleasantly surprised at how soft it was and how far down he sank. It sure was much nicer than the car seat he had been sitting on for so long. "It was fine," he replied, rubbing his hands on the arms of the chair.

The lawyer walked around the desk to sit in his own leather chair. "How long does it take to get up here from Lancaster?"

"About four hours with the road construction going on," Ben replied.

Mr. Lincoln's secretary brought a thick file into the office and laid it on the desk in front of him. After they had finished the small talk, the two men began going through all the papers in the file. The older gentleman explained each page to Ben before he signed it. Thomas Lincoln had known Ben's uncle for most of his life, and he was more than just his attorney—they were friends as well. Ben felt a little guilty that this man was much better acquainted with his uncle's life than he was. After a few hours, they had completed all of the necessary paperwork and needed to head down to the courtroom to procure a judge's signature, to make the transition of property complete. Once inside the elevator, they pressed the button and waited for the doors to close. Just as they began to slide shut, a large man's arm burst inside between the doors and pushed them back open. Three men in dark suits entered the elevator, speaking very loudly. They pushed into the car and backed the two men practically up against the rear wall. *How rude*, Ben thought to himself as he sized the men up. It was obvious by the appearance of their clothing and hand-sewn leather brief cases that they were not exactly poor men. The gentlemen did not acknowledge Ben or the attorney and continued to discuss a very large real estate venture that they were seeking permits for. Finally, the bell rang and the elevator doors opened to the courtroom floor. As the five men left the car and went in separate directions, Mr. Lincoln grabbed Ben's elbow and pulled him close, so he could speak in private. "Please promise me that you will not allow that man to get his hands on your uncle's property for any reason."

Ben looked confused at the gentleman. "Who is he?"

"His name is Silas Barnett." The attorney scowled as he said the name. "He is one of the richest men in the city. Got that way by swindling people mostly, and now he develops real estate. He is trying to buy up the homes in Willow Springs." He paused to look around, to ensure no one else was listening. "He wants to knock down the town and build some sort of resort around the hot springs for his rich friends up there. He plans on giving it to his spoiled brat son. When he finds out your uncle has passed, he will contact you and make an offer. Please do not sell to him."

Ben did not want to promise the attorney any such thing. He knew he had to sell his uncle's house, and if this gentleman was interested, why wouldn't he call the guy? He did not care if the town was there another hundred years, or if it was replaced by a spa. The town of Willow Springs had no sentimental value to him; it was just one more thing he had to deal with in his busy life.

It only took a few minutes for the judge to review and approve the estate paperwork, and then Ben was headed out of the courthouse with a map to his property in hand. He walked down to the river; it was beautiful. He closed his eyes for a moment to enjoy the warm breeze dancing across his face. He looked up and down the path in both directions to see if he could find his family. He called Diana's cell phone to find out what direction the giant dog had dragged her. A few minutes later, they met up down the path and sat for while watching kayakers on the water. Diana gave Barley as much leash as she could, hoping he would tire himself out and nap for the rest of the ride. After finally getting him stuffed back into the car, they headed back out of town to try and find their way to Ben's new house.

The road to Willow Springs was a long, windy, narrow one. Ben drove very slow, worrying what he would do if he encountered another vehicle coming from the other direction. There was no way the road was wide enough for two cars to pass, and with the deep forest on both sides, there was no place to pull over.

"Are you sure this is the way?" Diana asked. "This is more like a dirt path. How can there be a town up here?"

"I was thinking the same thing, but these are the directions Mr. Lincoln gave me. I think the town is all the way on top of the mountain." He slowed down even more to navigate the large ruts in the road that were caused by the pavement washing away. He worried that he would scrape the bottom of the car.

All of a sudden, Diana shouted and startled him quite a bit. "Ben, stop the car. I think I saw a bear."

Confused and startled, he slammed on the brakes. "Really, are you crazy?' he snapped. "You think there is a bear, and you want me to stop the car? And then what should I do? Get out of the car and poke at it? Shouldn't I drive faster, if there is really a bear?" Diana was not appreciating his tone or his sarcasm. She looked as though she was going to cry. He leaned over and pulled her close. He apologized and kissed her.

"You are not funny. I never saw a real live bear before. I was excited, and you ruined it," she said, almost in a pout. He laughed at her again. "It was a big bear." She leaned away and turned back toward her window.

He started maneuvering slowly through the bumps again. The trees were so thick that the space between them seemed pitch black. It was kind of spooky. Barley sat up and began to growl in a low, tone deep in his throat. *Great, now he's getting scared*, Ben thought to himself. *How will we ever sell this house if we can't even find the darn thing?* The car rocked side-to-side as they made their way up the winding road. Although it was only a few more miles, it seemed like they were driving forever.

The sun was setting when they finally arrived in the small town of Willow Springs. The young couple was absolutely shocked at how simple the town appeared. It felt as though they were stepping back in time.

"I think I saw this town on a postcard once," Diana said as she examined every house.

"Yeah, really," replied Ben, "from the 1800s, maybe."

As they slowly made their way up the main street, they could see the porch lights coming on and people peeking out of their windows to see who was disturbing the silence of their sleepy town.

"I don't suppose they get many visitors up here," Diana whispered and wrapped her arm around his.

They pulled into a parking spot in front of the café and went inside to get directions to his uncle's home. The café was empty except for a heavy-set woman behind the counter. She turned and looked surprised to see them. She looked them up and down for a moment, and then remembered her customer service skills and gave them a huge, warm country smile to welcome them.

"Hello there, come on in and sit down," she said as she placed two menus on the counter in front of them. "What can I get for you folks?" She was dying to ask them a ton of questions to find out who they were, where they were from, and what on earth had brought them to this tiny town.

The couple smiled and moved toward the counter. "Do you have a restroom that I could use to wash up?" asked Diana.

The woman nodded and pointed to the back. "Help yourself, honey." She then turned her attention to Ben as she poured two glasses of ice water and placed them on the counter. "Where you folks headed tonight?" She could no longer control her curiosity,

"Actually, right here." Ben smiled at her, knowing that she wanted more information. "Would you happen to know where I can find Dr. Bashore's house?"

"Oh, honey, I am so sorry. You are too late. Doc Bashore passed away a few weeks ago." She became distraught that she had to break such bad news.

Ben smiled to console her. "I know." He held out his hand to shake hers. "My name is Benjamin Bashore, and Doc Bashore was my uncle. My fiancée Diana and I are here to settle his estate."

Her face lit up with excitement, and she aggressively shook his hand. "Well, Benjamin Bashore, it is such a pleasure to meet you. My name is Sadie. I own this here establishment." She was speaking so fast that Ben could hardly keep up. "Doc Bashore was a dear, sweet man. Everyone in town adored him. We sure do miss him. Will you be moving into his house? What can we do to help?" she asked excitedly, sliding a basket of homemade dinner rolls in front of him.

Ben chuckled. She was moving way too fast for him at the moment. "Sadie, I am not sure how we are going to handle the estate at this moment, but we are here for the next two weeks to figure it out."

Diana returned and slid onto the stool next to Ben. Sadie made them a nice dinner and talked relentlessly throughout the entire process. She shared many stories about how Ben's uncle, Doc Bashore, helped the townspeople throughout the years. Ben listened intently to the tales of babies being delivered, broken bones being set, and illnesses being cured by his uncle. He learned that along with tending to the townsfolk for most of their lives, his uncle was also a deacon at the church and served on the town council until the day he passed away. The more the woman spoke, the closer he felt to his uncle. He had never realized what an integral part of this community his uncle had grown to be over the years. He was almost jealous of the close relationship this small-town doctor had developed with his patients. Ben's experience in the emergency room was very different. He treated strangers during their worst times, and then rarely saw them again after that. He looked forward to the day when he could have his own practice and get to know the families he was treating.

As she picked up the last of their dishes, Sadie tried once again to get Ben to consider moving to Willow Springs. "Sweetie, your uncle was a great man, and this town will not be the same without him."

Ben smiled proudly.

"We sure would appreciate if you would consider staying on and being our new Doc Bashore."

Ben smiled at Diana, who slid out of her chair and opened her bag to pull out her wallet. “It is getting really late, and it's been a long drive. We really should be getting to the house.”

Sadie gave them directions to Doc Bashore's house and invited them back for breakfast. She wrapped up some cinnamon buns for them to take with them, in case they got hungry later. The young couple was very impressed with her friendliness. As they turned to leave, she called them back and handed them another bag. “Take this for your friend out there. He looks hungry, too.”

They glanced out the window to see Barley standing on the front seat with his paws on the steering wheel, happily wagging his tail and spying in the diner window at them. They all chuckled.

“Thank you so much,” Diana said, taking the bag “I didn't even think about how we were going to feed him tonight.”

When they arrived back at the car, Ben grabbed the steering wheel to pull himself into the seat and his hand slipped off. “Aw, yuck, your dog slobbered all over my side of the car.”

Diana laughed at him and handed him some napkins from the bag. Ben grumbled as he wiped down the seat and steering wheel. “Ridiculous beast,” he whispered as he rubbed Barley’s head, and then backed the car out of the parking space and headed down the street toward the Bashore home.

“Wow, will you look at that?” Diana asked in amazement as they pulled up to the address the lawyer had given them. “Are you sure this is the right place?'

Ben just nodded and sat looking at the house for a moment. It was so much bigger than he expected it would be. It was a romantic-looking Victorian home with a nicely kept front lawn surrounded by a small black iron fence. There were curtains on all the windows, and night lights dimly lit up the interior. “It looks like someone still lives there,” Ben said.

“It looks creepy and haunted,” Diana replied quietly.

They sat for another moment, and then began unloading the car to head inside. Even though they were both completely exhausted, they spent the next hour exploring the entire house. Diana excitedly opened the doors to every room to learn the layout of the house, with Barley closely following behind her. Ben was more interested in the family pictures hung stylishly throughout each room. There were pictures of his parents and grandparents that he had never seen before. He fought back tears as he looked them over. He missed his parents very much and barely remembered his grandparents. He found a picture of himself as a small boy, sitting on the front porch of the house with Uncle Leonard. He must have been here before, but he had no recollection. *How could that be*, he thought to himself, *and why didn't I come here more and stay in touch with my uncle? He was my only family, and now it is too late.*

Diana returned to his side, but he had not noticed and it startled him when she spoke. “What are you doing?” she snapped quickly, and then giggled when he jumped a bit. “There are four bedrooms. What did your uncle need with four bedrooms if he never had children?”

“I don't know, but for us, that just means four more rooms of stuff to go through and figure out what to do with.” He handed her the picture of him and his uncle. She smiled and put her hand on his shoulder. Then he snapped back to the present moment. “We should probably take Barley outside for a few minutes before we turn in.”

"I got it," she said and skipped to the back door. "Come on, boy, let's go pee-pee." Barley excitedly bolted out the back door and ran across the yard to the tree line. Diana could not believe how dark and quiet it was in this town. The only sounds she heard were locusts chirping in the distance and Barley crashing through the brush, skipping excitedly from tree to tree. She sat on the back porch and waited for the dog to come back. Every few minutes she called out to Barley, trying to convince him to come in, but the dog continued to romp through the trees, chasing bugs and playing with the leaves.

Who knew that he liked being outside so much? she thought and pulled her sweater tightly around her shoulders. After about an hour, she finally talked the dog back into the house, and they settled in for the night.

CHAPTER SEVEN

THE NEXT MORNING THE SUN streamed through the window, past the lace curtains, across the bed, and finally met Diana's eyes to awaken her. She rolled over and reached out to find Ben, but he wasn't there. Surprised that he was up so early, she grabbed her robe and went to find him. As soon as she got downstairs, Barley was waiting for her at the door eagerly waiting to get back outside. She laughed and rubbed his head. "Let me get some coffee first, buddy." She glided into the kitchen, still wondering where Ben had gotten to, and poured herself a cup of coffee. Ben must be here somewhere, since there was coffee. She called out to him but received no answer. Barley whined and scratched at the door.

"Alright, alright, I will take you out and then find my boyfriend, you spoiled boy, you," she said sarcastically as she opened the back door. Barley pushed past her, almost knocking her down as he bolted toward the tree line to play. Diana sat down on the porch to wait. She admired the view from the back of the house. She could see miles upon miles of wavy hills covered in colorful trees, topped off by a brilliantly blue sky with white cumulus clouds. "My God, this town is so beautiful," she whispered. She stood up and began walking around the yard to see the outside of the house. On the left side of the house was a small room that appeared to be newer than the rest of the home. Doc Bashore had added this section onto the house years ago to serve as his office to see patients. It had separate entrances from the main house in the front and back. Diana noticed a light on and went over to peek into the back door. She was surprised to see Ben sitting at the desk, talking to a heavyset, middle-aged woman. Just then, the coffee mug in her hand accidentally tapped the glass of the window, and Ben looked up to see her. He smiled wildly and stood up to unlock the door and let Diana in.

"Honey, this is Berta," he began to introduce Diana when he realized she was still in her robe and stopped abruptly. "Why are you outside in your pajamas?"

"Hello, I am his fiancée, Diana." She reached out to shake the woman's hand, smiling, and then turned back to Ben. "I'm so embarrassed; I was taking Barley out when I saw the light. I did not know you had company."

The woman stood up and tried to ease her embarrassment. "It is fine, please do not worry. I worked with Doc Bashore for over twenty years, and believe me, I have seen much, much worse."

Diana felt relieved a bit and sat down next to Ben. "You worked with Uncle Leonard. Were you his assistant?" she asked.

Berta smiled. "Yep, his assistant, his nurse, his housekeeper, his landscaper, and best of all I had the pleasure of being his friend." They all smiled silently for a moment. "Your uncle was such a remarkable man, Ben. Everyone in town misses him so much."

Ben turned to Diana. "Berta stopped by to offer to help us with the estate. She knows every inch of the house well and is familiar with everything in it. She can really help us organize the stuff for the sale."

"Oh," Diana smiled once again to Berta. "That would be a huge help, we just don't know where to start."

"I will do whatever I can, but I have to admit that I would much rather be helping you two get settled into the town than to be selling off the doc's stuff to strangers."

"We only have two weeks off work, and then we have to return to Lancaster. We cannot stay here," Diana said apologetically. Just then Barley began barking outside, reminding her that she'd left him alone out there. "I better go get him. And maybe get some clothes on," she said, once again reaching for the woman's hand. "It was so nice to meet you, and we sure do appreciate your offer to help. I do hope we can talk more later."

"The pleasure is mine," responded Berta. She watched Diana go back outside, and then smiled to Ben. "She is a lovely woman, and you make such a beautiful couple. When is the big day?"

"We haven't set a date yet. We are both pretty busy at work right now. I refer to her as my wife sometimes already." Ben hesitated a bit. "I suppose one day we will just run off somewhere and officially tie the knot."

"Gotta make it official." Berta laughed. "I really wish there was a way you could stay on in Willow Springs and take over your uncle's practice." Ben just smiled. The idea was growing on him just a bit, but he had his job at Lancaster General, they had a lease on their apartment there, Diana had her teaching job, and her whole family was in Lancaster. He simply could not picture them living in such a rustic setting. Heck, he could not picture her living more than three miles from a shopping mall.

Ben and Berta spent many hours that day going through Doc Bashore's office and patient files.

"Where do you suggest that I should transfer these patient files to?" he asked Berta.

"I suppose the closest hospital is all the way down in Wilkes-Barre, but I don't imagine that anyone from town will travel down there. We will need to find us a new doctor right here in town, somehow." She thought for a few minutes. "Probably should be the patient's decision where they want their files. Can we box them up, and then ask everyone at the town meeting next Friday?"

Ben appreciated her input and agreed. "Alrighty then, we leave the files until Friday night and let the townsfolk decide. I like it." They continued to dig through the office, talk about the belongings, and share stories. The more they talked, the more Ben learned about his uncle, and the more he regretted not having a relationship with this great man.

Diana took a shower, got dressed, and busied herself organizing the kitchen. She made a list of a few groceries she thought they needed and headed over to the general store to pick them up. Afterward, she stopped by the diner to pick up some lunch for Ben, Berta, and herself. Once again Sadie packed a doggie bag for Barley. Everyone in town seemed to already know who she was. *I guess that's how it is in small towns,* she thought to herself. It certainly wasn't that way growing up in a city. She always felt invisible and alone. Everyone she spoke to here was very nice and genuinely listened when she spoke. She liked that a lot. But of course, they all were sure to drop a hint that the town really needed a doctor and hoped that Ben would decide to stay on. She grew tired of explaining her commitments back in Lancaster, so she began to simply thank them and smile.

The next couple of days went pretty much the same way. Ben and Berta rooted through the house, inventorying the contents of each room and sharing memories of Uncle Leonard. Diana took care of Barley, who wanted to spend most of his time in the woods, and helped with the packing as best she could. She took a trip to the general store each morning and stopped by the diner to chat with Sadie. In the evening, she and Ben would take Barely outside for his final romp through the brush while she relaxed on the porch swing, listening to the silence of the town.

"So, my love, what have you decided to do with this house and all the stuff inside?" she asked as she snuggled her head against Ben's chest.

He put his arm around her shoulder to keep her warm. "I just don't know yet." He was trying not to let her know how overwhelmed he was feeling with this entire project. "I've never had to deal with anything like this before."

"And...?" She paused, waiting for him to speak.

"And what?"

"And you are really enjoying finding all the pictures and family heirlooms. You are like a little boy on a treasure hunt."

They both laughed. He knew she was right. He was so infatuated by everything in the house that he had barely eaten or slept the past few days. "I'm sorry that I haven't spent more time with you. It's just that this house has brought me closer to my family than I've felt in a long time. I guess I didn't realize how lonely I have felt since my parents passed. Seeing the pictures here is bringing back so many great memories." He sat quietly for a moment, gently rocking the swing. "I just wish I would have made time to come visit him."

Diana reached up and touched his cheek. "I know, baby, I do too." After a moment, she tried to push him a bit more for his plan. "I noticed that you haven't really boxed a lot of stuff yet. I don't mean to be pushy, but do you have an idea of what you want to keep and what you want to sell? I mean, after all, we have to be back to our jobs in Lancaster in a little over a week."

Ben stood up and walked to the edge of the porch. "I know. It's just so hard. We can't have an auction, because the town would not want a lot of people to come up here. We can't take too many things back to our apartment because we don't have the room. We do not have time to sell this stuff individually, and I sure do not want to sell anything that has been in my family." He paused for another moment. "This is hard."

"I know, baby," she reassured him. She walked over to him and hugged him from behind. "I know."

They cuddled for a few minutes, and then she decided to make a suggestion. "What if you just keep the house and all his belongings, and come up when we get time off work? Sort of like a vacation home."

He spun around; he had not thought of that. That would be so much easier, he thought, but then the reality of the situation began to set in. "That would be amazing, but I just don't know if we could afford two households. We would still need to pay the utilities here and would need to hire someone to keep it clean. We will have to crunch some numbers to see if that is possible, but it is a great idea." He smiled, hugged her tightly, and kissed her forehead. "You are always the smart one."

She smiled proudly. "You are so right," she laughed. "Now go get your silly dog, and let's go into bed."

Diana could not fall asleep. The bed was soft and warm, the room was cool, and the pitter-patter of rain on the window made her very sleepy, but she just could not drift off. She listened to the rain tapping on the windowpane and the low roar of distant thunder and watched the white linens curtain dancing in the breeze. Growing up in the city, she had never taken the time to just lie back and listen to a storm. She was amazed at how calming and beautiful it could be.

Life was so different here. Everything seemed so much simpler and far less stressful. There was no traffic, no loud neighbors, no barking dogs, no trains bustling through town. Just the quiet sounds of nature to lull her to sleep. It was more than that, though, that she admired about this little town. Everyone was so friendly and genuinely seemed to care about their neighbors. It was as if the entire town was one big family for generations that worked together to take care of everyone who lived there. She thought about how they all welcomed her and Ben immediately and made sure they did not feel like outsiders. It had been a long time since Diana had felt like she was part of a group.

A bright flash of lightning illuminated the room, followed by a long rumble of thunder, making Barley roll over and whine from his closet. *How can such a big dog be afraid of so much?* she thought. She rolled onto her side and pulled the comforter up over her shoulders. Ben was sound asleep and snoring as loud as the thunder. She wondered how much time he had spent here with his uncle as a child. She had never been out of the city. She thought about their apartment in Lancaster and realized how much time she actually spent there alone—well, almost alone, she did have Barley. Ben worked so many hours at the hospital. They knew that long hours were a requirement during his residency, but that didn't make it easier. Diana worked full-time at the elementary school and usually had hours of work to do at home creating projects and grading papers for the next day. Up until a week ago, she had loved her life and was very happy. Lying there now, she feared how lonely she would be to return to that small apartment and busy city schedule. How could she ever tell Ben such a thing? He was doing so well at the hospital, and she was very proud of him. He'd worked so hard to get where he was. It just would not be fair to ask him to change his life so drastically now. Maybe it would have been better if she never came to Willow Springs. Another flash of lightning and the soft breeze streaming through the window finally put her to sleep.

In the morning when she woke, Ben and Barley were already gone. The room was so chilly, it was tough to pull off the blankets and get up. It just felt like a great day to stay in bed, but there was too much to do. Eventually she slid out from under the warm blanket, grabbed her robe, and closed the window. She had to laugh a bit as she saw Ben being dragged across the backyard by Barley. By the time she was dressed and made it downstairs, Ben had given up trying to get Barley back inside the house.

"He is getting much harder to love," Ben joked as he leaned over to kiss her.

"Would you like me to take over waiting for him?" Ben nodded and headed for the kitchen, leaving the door to the yard wide open. "I'll close that for you," she whispered sarcastically. As she reached for the handle something at the edge of the trees caught her eye. She was sure that she saw a woman looking out of the forest toward the house. As their eyes met, the woman backed up until she was hidden in the brush. "Hello," Diana called out, but there was no response. She reached down to slide a pair of slippers onto her feet, grabbed a sweater from the coat rack, and walked out to the edge of the yard. Looking through the trees, she did not see anyone or any indication that anyone had been through the area recently. She stood very still for a moment, and then giggled to herself. *Wow, I must be getting as crazy as that silly dog.*

As she turned to return to the house, she heard branches breaking a few feet away, as if someone was walking through the forest. "Hello," she called out again, "is someone there? Hello!" No one answered her, but she could hear the footsteps getting farther away. She carefully began to make her way through the thick brush to follow the sound. Every few moments, she would stop and listen to make sure she was going the right way and continued to call out, but there was never a response. She began to worry that it could be an animal she was following, and suddenly it dawned on her that the animal could actually be stalking her. She began to panic and thought about turning back. Then she saw the woman again for a brief second as she climbed over a large rock. She had only seen her from the back, but she now knew that she definitely was not following an animal. The woman had long black hair and was wearing a long, tan dress and no shoes. Diana was intrigued and began to move faster through the brush on her pursuit. She simply had to know who this woman was and why she was out walking with no shoes. "Please wait, I just want to talk to you." She pushed on for what seemed like a very long time. She was thinking how crazy it was that she was getting deeper into the forest, wearing her slippers, following a stranger, and not sure if she could ever find her way back to the house.

Suddenly she pushed through some thick brush and came upon a clearing that was on the edge of a cliff. She was astonished by the view from the little clearing. It overlooked the huge valley, and she could see miles upon miles of rolling hills filled with green trees. It appeared to go on forever and was simply amazing. She had never felt so close to God as she did at that moment. Someone had split a log in half and made a tiny bench a few feet into the clearing, so she sat down and took a deep breath. As she inhaled, the air smelled clean and fresh, as if everything had been washed anew by the rain the evening before. It was so peaceful and relaxing. She just sat quietly for a long while looking out over miles and miles of pure nature. It felt as though she was the only one on the planet, until she felt a hand on her shoulder. Startled, she jumped to her feet with a small scream.

"Oh, ma'am, I am so sorry. I didn't mean to frighten you." Ned Ferguson, the general store owner, grabbed her hand to calm her down. "I called out to you, but I guess you did not hear me. I apologize for giving you such a fright." He motioned with his hand to ask permission to join her on the bench as she slid back down into her seat. She nodded her approval and began telling him the story of how she'd followed the mystery woman through the forest and ended up here. At first, she worried about how crazy it must sound as she said it out loud, and then it dawned on her: where could the woman have possibly gone? *She was in front of me the entire time, there is no place to turn off, and she isn't in the clearing.* Diana was tempted to look over the edge of the steep cliff for a moment, and then realized that notion was insane.

"Are you alright?" Ned asked.

Realizing that she had stopped speaking mid-sentence, she looked at his face to see if she could read how crazy he must have thought she was. He didn't appear shocked at all at her disappearing woman story—he seemed to be still listening intently, waiting to hear what had happened next. She nodded to let him know she was alright and continued on with her crazy story. When she finished, she paused and waited for his reaction.

He patted her hand, and then stood up to walked to the edge of the cliff. She followed him. Pointing to the right, to an area below the cliff that had a great deal of steam rising from it, he asked, "See down there? That entire side of the mountain is covered in natural hot springs. They are not supposed to exist in Pennsylvania, but there they are." He turned to look her directly in the eyes. "Anyone who ain't seen them, may not believe they are here. Sometimes you just see stuff that no one else is going to believe, but that's okay. It doesn't mean you are crazy." He smiled warmly and patted her on the shoulder.

She appreciated his comments but still felt silly. "Does anyone from town ever use the hot springs?"

"Sure do. You follow that path right there down the hill. It gets a little tricky around the second turn, but it takes you right to them. Best cure on the planet for whatever ails you." He smiled at her and returned to the little bench, and then bent down to rub his right knee. "Unfortunately, Fat Cat Silas Barnett wants to force everyone out of town so he can buy up the entire mountain and turn it into some sort of fancy health spa for the rich."

"That's awful. Hasn't the town been here for generations?" Diana asked. "No one would really sell to him, would they?"

"Most of the houses have been in the same family for over two hundred years," he explained. "That is why it is so important to many of us that Ben doesn't sell his uncle's house to some stranger." He watched her face for some indication of her plans for the property. When she remained silent, he added "Or if you have to sell her, we will just have to get used to it." He smiled and gave her a small wave, and then reminded her to be careful returning through the forest. He turned and headed into the trees. Just at the edge of the forest, he turned to share one last thought. “For the record, ma’am, I have seen the native woman a few times myself.” Then he disappeared.

I never said she was a Native American, she thought to herself.

Back at the house, she found Ben hard at work sorting through his uncle’s belongings once again. She decided not to tell him about the woman but did share the fact that she’d found an amazing spot to sit and enjoy the nature around them. She also told him about the hot springs and how real estate developers were trying to pressure the townspeople into selling their homes.

“And you did all of this in your bedroom slippers?” Ben chuckled as he leaned over and kissed her head on his way past her.

She looked down at her feet. Her slippers were muddy and torn. Fantastic, she thought and headed upstairs to change them.

The next morning, Ben decided to take a break from rummaging through the house and join Diana and Barley on their daily walk into town. They took the long way around the streets to get more familiar with the town's layout and check out the magnificent views that surrounded them.

“This town is amazing,” Ben whispered to Diana. “It is almost like time forgot these people. They have isolated themselves from the rest of the world and live like people did a hundred years ago.”

Diana laughed. “They have electricity and indoor plumbing and some other modern conveniences. It is just that they have chosen to be a strong, tight-knit community, and to take care of each other. It is very quaint.” They headed for the general store. Diana ran in to grab a few supplies for the day, while Ben sat on the porch with Barley. The dog was very excited and happily greeted everyone that walked by. Ben was charmed by how friendly everyone in the town was toward him and Diana. Without fail, each person who stopped for a minute to greet them and pat Barley's head would subtly drop a hint that the town hoped Ben would decide to take over his uncle's practice and stay on as the new town doctor.

Diana emerged from the store, smiling. She had a basket draped over her forearm and was swinging her hips dramatically as she walked. "Look, Ben, Mr. Ferguson gave me this basket to bring back each day to carry my groceries. Isn't that sweet?"

"Well, you look absolutely stunning with your little basket," he chuckled. "Just like my Grandma used to shop." She smacked him and laughed. They headed over to the diner to grab some sandwiches for lunch. Barley would not be happy if they forgot to pick up the goodie bag that Sadie packed for him each day.

As they approached the diner, a small girl with a long dark braid and dark skin walked out from behind a corner. Barley adored children, and as soon as he saw her, he became so excited that he pulled the leash from Ben's unsuspecting hand. The dog bolted straight at the little girl and knocked her flat on her back to lick her face. The girl cried out loudly, and the couple ran to her aid. Ben grabbed the leash and pulled the dog away. Diana picked up the little girl and wiped her face. "Sweetheart, we are so sorry. Are you alright?"

Xuan was fiercely angry. She glared at the dog with a laser stare. Barley whimpered and cowered down behind Ben's legs, almost knocking him down. "What on earth, Barley, now you are afraid of the little girl? What has gotten into you, silly dog?"

Diana gently turned Xuan's face toward her so that she could wipe the tears from her eyes. Suddenly the girl reached out and touched Diana's hair. She caressed her tiny hand down the side of the woman's cheek. Diana's Hispanic complexion was the first non-white skin the little girl had seen since she left her own village. She hugged Diana tightly and cried for a few minutes. This stranger reminded her of her mother, who she had been missing terribly for many, many years.

Sadie came running out of the diner. "Xuan," she cried out. Diana reassured her that the little girl was unhurt. She grabbed Xuan and spun her around to look directly into her face. "Honey, the dog did not mean to hurt you, it was an accident. These are very nice people, and they would be very upset if anything happened to their dog. They love him very much."

Diana and Ben thought this was odd and just looked at each other. Ben shrugged his shoulders to indicate that he did not understand what Sadie was trying to say. Barley peeked through Ben's legs to see what the women were doing but whimpered again when Xuan looked at him.

Sadie stood up and took the girl's hand. "Come on, guys, let's all get some lunch," she said and motioned for them to join her in the diner. Once inside, Xuan went into the back to play, and the two adults slid up to counter. Diana placed her basket on the floor between their stools. As Sadie prepared their lunches, she shared more stories with Ben about his uncle. "He was such a major part of our town," she said softly. "We miss him greatly."

As they ate, there was a long period of silence. Both Diana and Ben were eager to ask Sadie about the little native girl and her strange reaction to the girl's crying but wanted to find the correct words to not sound rude. Suddenly, Ben just blurted out the question, "Sadie, where did that little girl come from? She looks to be Native American."

Sadie chuckled, as she knew the question was inevitable but thought perhaps the topic would come up more subtly. "Xuan sort of belongs to our town. We all take care of her." The couple were still confused and sat patiently waiting for more information. "She is an orphan. Her parents were killed a while back, and we adopted her. Everyone in town helps to take care of her."

"Why were you concerned that something would happen to Barley?" asked Diana.

"Bad things tend to happen when Xuan becomes upset." Sadie paused. "Sometimes, bad things happen. There is nothing to worry about, he will be fine." Feeling a bit nervous and not wanting to share any more about their little mystery girl, she tried to change the subject. "Who is ready for some pie? I have fresh baked apple pie, and it is still warm."

The couple turned down the pie but did sit for quite a while longer, drinking coffee and chatting with the diner patrons. Ben enjoyed hearing about his uncle's adventures. Everyone in the town had a story about how Dr. Bashore had taken care of them or helped them out. Ben was proud that his uncle was such a good man at heart. The more stories he listened to, the more he regretted not making the time to visit him. As they packed up to head back to work at the house, Sadie once again made her daily pitch to Doctor Ben, reminding him how badly the town needed a new doctor and how much they all wanted him to stay. Ben just smiled and thanked her for the goodie bag she'd packed for Barley.

The minute they were out of the diner and headed down the road home, Diana was bursting to talk about Xuan. "What in the world is going on here?" she blurted. "Did you see the little girl's dress? It is made from some sort of leather that looks like animal hide. Where did she come from?"

Ben tried to explain, "Diana, there are still Native American tribes in the area. It is not that strange."

"Yeah, okay, silly. Of course there are still Native American tribes, but they dress in modern-day clothes, not animal skins."

That was a good point, he thought to himself but didn't want to admit to her. It was a little strange. "She looked like she was at least six or seven years old. I wonder why she isn't in school with the other kids."

"Good question. I would ask Sadie tomorrow, but she didn't really look like she wanted to talk about her anymore, did she? Hey, I am kind of full, let's take a walk around and explore the town a little bit to work off some of the calories we just ate," she suggested. She knew that Ben would go right back to digging through his uncle's belongings when they got back to the house, and she would be bored. So, they walked hand-in-hand, admiring the antique architecture of the homes, some of which were over a hundred years old. The town seemed to have everything that it needed to take care of its citizens. The couple circled around the entire town and then sat by the lake for a while, talking and skipping rocks across the shimmery surface of the water. Ben lay back on the grassy bank and thought to himself, *when was the last time we were both this relaxed?* Barley flopped down next to him and snuggled up for a nap, and the afternoon drifted away.

Finally, Diana was ready to head back to the work they had waiting for them at the house, and they slowly made their way back to path that led to their new backyard. As they approached the back door, Berta came busting out. "Dr. Bashore, please come quickly. One of the school teachers brought a student into the office. He fell and is bleeding pretty badly." Without hesitation, Ben handed Barley's leash to Diana and disappeared through the office door. Once inside, he found a small boy crying dramatically and holding his forearm. Ben knelt down so he was eye-level with the boy. "Hello, buddy, I am Doctor Ben, what is your name?"

The boy stopped crying. "Tommy," he muttered. After a few sniffles, he added his last name. "Tommy Martin"

"Well, Tommy Martin, it is a pleasure to meet you." He slowly lifted the towel that was wrapped around Tommy's arm and asked, "What happened here?"

Tommy sniffled some more and explained that he had fallen off the jungle gym and must have cut his arm on the way down.

"There must be a loose bolt on the jungle gym that he cut his arm on. I picked him up right away and ran here. Can you help him?" asked Mrs. Kramer, Tommy's teacher.

"Well, Tommy, you are going to need a few stitches, but we will get you all fixed up in no time." Ben stood up and patted Tommy on the head. "Berta, can you clean the wound while I get the supplies we will need?" Then he turned to the teacher. "Ma'am, where are Tommy's parents? I am going to need to speak with them to get permission to treat the boy."

The teacher was a bit confused. Dr. Bashore never worried about obtaining permission; he just went ahead and treated everyone who needed it. "We called for his mother; she is on her way over. Do you really need to wait for her? Can't you just help him?"

Just then the door burst open and a frantic woman exploded into the room, calling out for Tommy.

Ben held out his hand to the woman. "You must be Tommy's mom. I am Ben Bashore. He is fine." She shook his hand and began to calm down. "Yes, I'm his mother. You can call me Kendra."

"It is nice to meet you, Kendra. Tommy will need a few stitches in his arm. It is nothing serious, but I do need your permission to proceed."

"Of course, please take care of him." She bent down at Tommy's side and held his hand for support.

As Ben and Berta prepared to fix Tommy's arm, Diana invited his mom and teacher into the kitchen for some coffee. Ben appreciated her taking them away to give him more room to work. The women immediately hit it off and began to talk endlessly. Mrs. Kramer was thrilled to discover that Diana too was a teacher. She invited her to visit the schoolhouse and meet the children. "You know," she whispered, moving closer to Diana, "we are understaffed at the school and could really use another full-time teacher to help out."

Mrs. Martin nodded her head in agreement. "It would be so great if you and Ben stayed here in Willow Springs with us."

"And it would be such a shame for this big, beautiful home to sit empty," added Mrs. Kramer. Before Diana could explain to the ladies that they already had jobs back in Lancaster, Tommy emerged from the office with a bandage on his arm and a smile on his face. "Look, Momma, my arm is all better now."

Ben followed behind him. "Well, it's not all better, but it will be. He will need to come back in a week to get the stitches out," he said. Then he knelt down to Tommy again. "Try to keep your bandage clean for me, will ya, sport?" Tommy agreed and ran outside. His mom could not thank the doctor enough. She was so relieved that he had taken care of her son. Ben gave her a bag with some extra bandages to take home with her. As the women went toward the door to leave, Ben promised the teacher that he would bring some tools to the school and look into fixing the bolt that Tommy had cut himself on. She was very grateful.

After the women left, Diana grabbed Ben, wrapped her arms around his neck, and gave him a big kiss. "You are such a good guy," she said, leaning back to look into his eyes. "You are my hero."

"I love being your hero, but that was nothing special, just a few stitches. I literally do that all night long at the ER in Lancaster. Sixteen hours straight most nights." He blew it off, but in his head, he agreed. Even though he had stitched hundreds of wounds before, somehow this was different. Somehow it seemed more personal, more important, more special. Berta knew it had gotten to him. She smiled, hoping that the good doctor was beginning to warm up to the idea of living in Willow Springs.

They all went into the office to clean up the mess left from the emergency. Diana noticed a small drawer built into the wall between two bookshelves. She tried to pull it open to look inside, but it was locked. "Ben, did you find a key for this drawer?"

He and Berta both laughed at her. "No, sweetheart, that is our mystery drawer. It is the only place in the house that Berta was not allowed to go, and we cannot find the key for it. It has been driving us crazy for days trying to figure it out."

Diana was intrigued. "We could pry it open, couldn't we?"

"No, we are not going to risk damaging the wood. You will just have to be patient and help us find the key, silly girl," Ben teased her. She continued to try and pull the drawer open for a few minutes, but it wouldn't budge, so she spent the rest of the day searching through the house high and low for the magical key that would open the mysterious locked drawer.

Later that evening, just after Berta had gone home, there was a knock on the back door. Ben opened it, thinking that Berta had forgotten something and came back. Instead he found a rugged man standing outside, holding a large pot covered in aluminum foil.

"Good evening," the gentleman said a bit nervously. "I am Albert Martin." He struggled to juggle the pot and hold out his hand to the doctor.

"Oh, yes, you must be Tommy's father," Ben responded

"Yes, my wife and I wanted to thank you for taking care of our boy. She made you this stew, and my boys and I stacked enough cut wood in your yard to get you through the winter." He handed Ben the pot.

Ben was a bit shocked at how heavy the pot was and quickly set it on the counter, so as to not drop it. "Wow, that is a whole lot of stew." He smiled at the man and looked past him out into the yard. "And a whole lot of wood. You didn't need to do this, it was my pleasure to help Tommy." He was trying to figure out in his head how they'd stacked all that wood in the yard without Diana or himself hearing a thing. "Really, this wasn't necessary."

"That is the way it has always worked in Willow Springs. Doc Bashore always took care of us, and we paid him with services and food. Jasper fixes his car, Henry works on the house. The wives cook for him and do his laundry, and our kids take care of his yard work. I am the town lumberjack of sorts. I own a small lumber business, and I supply everyone in town with wood for their stoves. It is how we get through the winter. I am sorry if it isn't enough—it is all we have to pay with. The town doesn't have a lot of money, so we take care of each other."

Diana was listening in and sensed that her husband had somehow offended Mr. Martin, so she jumped into the conversation. "Well, thank you so much. We are overwhelmed by your family's generosity. You have done so much, and we greatly appreciate it. You are very kind." She smiled warmly and grasped his hand between both of her own. The man thanked her again and headed back out through the yard to leave. Ben and Diana went out to the edge of the porch to look at the massive pile of cut wood they now had. She placed her arm around Ben and smiled playfully at him. "Well, babe, we now have enough wood to get us through the winter. What do you think about that?"

Ben chuckled. "We won't be here in the winter."

Diana smiled warmly and hugged him tightly. "I know, but I am just so impressed with the generosity of these people. They are so close and caring. I had no idea that towns like this still existed. It's like they jumped off the pages of a history book or something."

Ben nodded in agreement. "It certainly is different than living in the city." They snuggled for a while, watching the full moon slowly sneak out from behind the timberline and inch its way toward the highest point of the night sky. After a while, Diana realized that she had not taken Barley out for his evening walk, so she went in the house to find him. She searched the house and called out to him but could not find him. This is odd, she thought, the silly mutt loves to be outside. She finally found him curled up in the bedroom closet upstairs. Try as she may, she could not convince him to come outside. Finally, she gave in. "Alright, Barley," she said, patting his head, "you stay cuddled up in here for the night, and we will go out in the morning. I am pretty worn out tonight too."

The next morning, Diana continued her search for the missing key that would open the mysterious locked drawer. Her curiosity was getting the best of her. Uncle Leonard had so many intriguing belongings all over the house, and his personal and financial information was openly available in his desk. It did not appear that any of his valuables were hidden or locked up, so what could possibly be so important to him that it was hidden in the locked drawer? She really wanted to find out.

Ben convinced Barley to finally go outside, but he did his business and quickly returned to the house. He did not want to play or romp through the woods like he normally did. He ran back through the door and hid under a table. *Why is this dog acting so strangely? Well, at least he isn't making messes in the house,* Ben thought to himself as he headed back into the office to continue his work.

After a while, Diana grabbed her basket and headed to the general store for her daily shopping trip. When she arrived, there was a large box truck parked outside. *This must be their weekly delivery truck that brings the town their supplies and mail,* she thought. Sadie had explained to her that was how the business in town received their products.

There were several large men working quickly to unload the heavy boxes from the truck. Some of the cases were going into the general store, some were headed over to the diner, and others were being handed off to people waiting on the sidewalk for the packages they were expecting. When she entered the store, she met Henry the delivery driver. He was an older gentleman. He made her feel a bit uneasy, because he stood way too close and liked to put his hand on women's shoulders or arms as he spoke to them. He told her that there was a package of medical supplies on the truck that Ben's uncle had ordered a while back and asked one of the men to bring it in the store to her. "Or if you like, ma'am, I could personally deliver it to the house for you," he said in a soft tone, leaning very close to her.

"Oh, no thank you. That's very kind of you, but my husband will take care of it." She backed away from him and continued her shopping. Ben had been working so hard going through the house the past few days, so she decided that she would cook him a special dinner later that evening. That is, if she could convince him to take a few minutes to just sit and relax for a while. After all, this was the only time they would get this year that was anything like a vacation. She was carefully making her way through the store, selecting her ingredients, when she bumped into one of the school teachers.

"You really should stop by the school and meet our students," the woman suggested. "We would love to hear your thoughts on our program. It is always good to get feedback from others in the profession, and quite frankly, we do not get many visitors in our little town."

Diana actually liked the idea and was curious about how this small-town education system worked. She was happily planning her visit when she noticed Henry through the front store window. He was standing outside the store, talking to Xuan. An uneasy feeling grew quickly inside her and she lifted her heavy basket onto the shelf. She turned toward the teacher.

"Tomorrow morning works great. I am looking forward to seeing your program. Will you please excuse me?" she muttered quickly as she turned away and sped to the front of the store. By the time she made it out the door, Henry and Xuan had disappeared.

"Oh, this is not good," she said out loud, looking up and down the small street. She called out to an elderly couple who were making their way to the front of the general store. "Excuse me, have you seen Xuan?" They shook their heads. Diane began to panic, not even knowing why she was so concerned. She ran down the alley between the buildings and slid around the corner to the back of the general store. There she found Henry leaning down in front of Xuan with his hands on her shoulders. By the look on his face, she knew that he was up to something despicable. Diana grabbed Henry's wrist hard and yanked him away from the small girl.

"Xuan, go in the store," Diana said, glaring at Henry. Xuan grabbed a hold of Diana's shirt and wanted to stay with her. "Sweetheart, please go in the store and wait for me. I will be there in a minute and we will get some ice cream." She tried to smile at Xuan, but she was so angry with Henry, she simply couldn't fake a smile. Xuan slid around the corner slowly but did not go into the store. She peeked back around the corner to ensure that Diana was going to be alright.

Diana turned her angry glare toward Henry. She squeezed his wrist as hard as she could and held it up in the air in front of his face.

"If you ever touch that little girl again, you will lose this hand. Do you understand me?" she growled.

"Oh, you are a feisty one, aren't you? I like that." Henry moved closer to her. She could not believe how disgusting this man could be. Obviously, he wasn't receiving her message, and she was angrier than she had ever been in her life. She was in no way a violent person, but she had had enough. She moved toward him and raised her knee as hard as she possibly could, striking him in the genitals. He let out a loud groan and dropped to the ground in pain.

"I'm telling the sheriff about this, and you better believe that I am calling the company your work for, you disgusting pervert." Diana kicked dirt at him and turned to leave. Xuan quickly ran up the alley, trying to make it into the store before Diana saw that she'd disobeyed her order. As promised, she and Xuan shared some ice cream as Diana discussed the Henry situation with the shop owner. He assured her that he would take care of contacting the supply company to get a new driver. Xuan stroked Diana's long dark hair as she squirmed around on the stool, eating her ice cream cone.

The shop owner smiled. "I believe someone really likes you, Diana. Perhaps you remind her of her mother."

Diana smiled.

Henry rolled around in the dirt, trying to recover from the pain enough to get to his feet. Once he could walk, he ran to his truck as quickly as he could, slammed the rear door shut and left the town.

That bitch, he thought to himself, *why couldn't she mind her own damn business?* "It's okay, Henry," he said out loud to himself, "she is a stranger in town, and that kid don't talk. If she tells anyone, I will simply deny it. No one will believe her. She is from the city." He convinced himself that everything was going to be alright and relaxed a bit. He lit a cigarette and turned up the radio. He was driving down the beat-up road faster than he had ever done before, and the empty truck was bouncing through the potholes hard, making a thunderous booming sound on every bump. He just wanted to get far away from Willow Springs as fast as he could. He puffed on the cigarette again, swerving around the turns of the windy road. The truck was thumping loud from every bump in the road. He swung the wheel hard to navigate a sharp right turn and immediately saw a clump of black fur crossing the road. He slammed on the brakes and turned the wheel hard in the opposite direction to try and avoid hitting the large animal. His cigarette fell on his lap, and he took his eyes off the road trying to brush it off before he got burned. The front of the truck struck the side of an old iron bridge, and the tire immediately exploded. The big truck skidded back and forth across the road, and it took all of Henry's strength to keep it from rolling over. He held on to the wheel as hard as he could and practically had to stand on the brake pedal to get the big truck to skid safely to a stop.

As soon as the truck had stopped and he realized that he was safe, he began to punch the steering wheel and let out a long string of curses. He could not believe the awful day he was having. It was getting dark, and he was broken down on the side of the road, miles from anywhere. There was no chance that anyone would be traveling that road for days. He slid out of the truck, still frustrated, and punched the side of the door in anger, hurting his hand. Things just were not getting better for him. He slid around the side of the truck to assess the damage. Part of the bumper was torn off; there were dents throughout the entire truck. He knew that he was going to be in a great deal of trouble from his boss, but right now, he was only concerned with getting the truck to move so he could get out of the dark woods. The tire had exploded and the wheel was bent, but he thought that if he could change the tire, he may be able to drive the truck slowly back to the city and get the rest repaired there.

He knew that it would get dark very quickly, and he only had a few moments to get the bad tire replaced. He was struggling to get anything done with the pain in his hand from punching the truck. *I am such an idiot at times,* he thought. As he opened the back of the truck to pull out the spare, he heard a long, low growl come from the edge of the trees. At first he was scared. He took his flashlight and shined it into the woods to check between every tree for any signs of an animal. When he did not see anything, he convinced himself that it was nothing, and he was just being jumpy.

"Stop acting like some scared chick," he commanded himself out loud.

He struggled to drag the spare tire up to the front of the truck and knelt down to start working the jack. Suddenly he heard crackling sounds coming from directly behind him, like someone was walking toward him through the brush. Again, he shined the flashlight in the trees. He stood up and walked toward the edge of the road, waving his arms and making loud shooing noises to try and scare any animals away. When it was silent, he returned to working on the tire. The sun had set, and it was quickly becoming darker every minute now. The woods were pitch black, and the only light that Henry could see for miles was coming from his tiny flashlight. Even though he was a big, tough man, he had to admit that he was scared. Anything could happen to a person out here in these woods, and it would be several days before anyone would ever find him. He worked as fast as he could, spinning the lug nuts off the bad tire and trying to unbend the wheel. He finally pulled the bad tire free and turned to grab the new tire so he could finish the repair and get out of the dark. He pointed the flashlight at where he'd left the spare, but there was nothing there. "What the hell?" he yelled out loud. He knew that he had dragged the tire to the front of the truck and dropped it right there. He shined the light around the entire area but could not find it. *Maybe I am losing my freaking mind and I didn't get it out of the truck,* he thought, even though he knew that he had. He stood up to walk to the back of the truck and heard a loud thump. Something had hit the other side of the truck so hard that the box was shaking back and forth. Henry stumbled back a few steps and stood in shock. He was terrified now. He could not move or make a sound; he was literally scared stiff.

It was all he could do to get air in his lungs. *What the hell is going on here? Something is behind my truck.* He could feel his heart pounding in his chest. He decided to make a run for the truck, planning to lock himself in the cab until morning, but as soon as he took a step, he tripped and fell. The flashlight went flying out of his hand and smashed to the ground. Now there was nothing but darkness. He heard another long, low growl. He was so scared that he pulled his knees to his chest and began to cry. He could hear deep breathing coming closer and closer to him. His body was shaking violently. He thought about getting up and running for the truck again but could not make his body move. He felt a tuft of fur brush against his leg. He tried to scream, but no sound came out. He felt hot breath waft across his face. His chest tightened. He waved his hands to discover who was there but found nothing. He closed his eyes tightly again and began to cry. Then suddenly he felt the excruciating pain of teeth biting through his flesh. He lifted his arm to see a stub without a hand. His hand was gone. At that moment, the shock and pain overtook him, and he passed out.

A few days later, the supply truck arrived early. Ned came out of his general store to greet the new driver and find out why the delivery day had changed. He was not prepared to unload product today. The driver explained that Henry was no longer with the company, and that he would be taking over the delivery route. Ned was surprised by Henry's sudden career change and joked with the young man that he must have won the lottery and retired to an exotic island somewhere.

"No sir," the new driver answered as he began to grab boxes off his truck. "Unfortunately, his truck broke down, and he was attacked by a wild animal in the woods. Rumor has it that he lost his hand."

Everyone was shocked to hear such a story.

"I would really like to unload each week and be down that windy road before dark sets in, if it's all the same to you folks." Ned nodded and grabbed some boxes to help.

Diana recalled her threat behind the market when she heard the story. Although she knew that she could not have possibly caused the coincidental accident involving Henry's hand, she did feel a bit guilty for saying such a thing in the first place. She wasn't disappointed that he would no longer be on the delivery route, though. She was happy that the town would not have to put up with his inappropriate advances.

CHAPTER EIGHT

EDWARD MORNINGSTAR HAD BEEN a tenured professor at Tremble University for more years than he could recall. He developed the Native American History department and had introduced many Philadelphia students to the true history of the original inhabitants of what is now known as the state of Pennsylvania. It was not his original intention to teach others about native history when he began to research his heritage so intently. You see, he was born on the Lapoui Reservation located in Utah and was simply trying to understand his own heritage. The more he discovered about the history of his people, the more he wanted to share with anyone that would listen. Becoming a Native American History teacher just seemed to be a natural progression for him.

Dr. Leonard Bashore had contacted the professor several times with an incredible story about a Native American who lived in his town. While he had repeatedly discussed the matter for multiple hours on the phone, and the doctor had sent him files of data on the case, Edward was not convinced that the story of the little girl was for real. After consulting with many of his fellow American History scholars, he was planning a trip up to the village of Willow Springs to meet with the doctor and the little girl, but had learned of his passing before he could arrange time off work. When the summer classes ended, he decided to make the trip anyway, hoping to find this mysterious native girl who supposedly never aged.

It was only about a six-hour drive north to the town of Wilkes-Barre. Professor Morningstar figured that someone there could direct him the rest of the way to Willow Springs. He loaded up his 1972 El Camino with a few essentials and set out on his adventure. It was a scenic drive up the turnpike and through the mountains. The valleys were in full bloom, and as the sun sparkled down on the mountains behind them, it lit up the trees into bright colors. It had been quite a while since he had time to get out of the city, and he had almost forgotten how beautiful the state of Pennsylvania is in the summer. Once he made it to Wilkes-Barre, he stopped at a local diner to grab a drink, use the restroom, and get directions for the rest of his journey. The waitress found the professor very intriguing, so she included her phone number on the same napkin that she jotted down the directions for him. As he started up the long dirt road that led to Willow Springs, he thought she was playing a joke on him.

This can't be the right way, this is barely even a road, he thought. He made his way through the potholes and deep ruts in the road at a very slow pace. He did not want to bounce his precious vintage car and was trying hard not to get it dirty. He was pretty certain that he was not going to encounter any other vehicles on this path, so going at such a slow pace was not likely to hold anyone else up. The farther up the dusty trail he went, the more he was concerned that the waitress was sending him out to the middle of nowhere. *This has got to be the wrong road*, he kept repeating to himself. As he gently maneuvered his front tires through a rut in the road, a sudden movement caught his eye. High up in the top of a tall pine tree sat a huge bird looking down at him. Edward thought that the bird was probably laughing at his driving, and then he realized that it was an eagle. He was in awe, because he had never seen an eagle in the wild. He quickly stopped the car and grabbed his cell phone to take a picture of the majestic creature. Just as he clicked the shutter, the bird swooped down out of the tree toward his car, and then quickly made a sharp turn and flew low to the ground directly up the road and disappeared around a turn. The man was still in awe. That moment alone made the drive worth his time.

"Alright, my friend, if you say this is the right way, I will follow," he said out loud, as if the bird could possibly hear him. So, he jumped back into the car and continued his slow-paced journey, meticulously maneuvering around the bumps and holes until he finally reached the town.

Once there, he introduced himself to the local people in an attempt to get acquainted with how this tiny town functioned. All the while, he was looking around for a little Native American girl. He did not mention his research or the wild story that Dr. Bashore had shared with him at first. He told them that he was a friend of the doctor's and was asked to visit Xuan, to see if he could identify her tribe. No one suspected any different. When Sadie heard his story, she sent a young boy to fetch Ben. Ben and the professor hit it off immediately and spent several hours sitting in a booth, talking about Ben's uncle, the town, Native American history, and the only little road that led to Willow Springs. Near the end of their conversation, the professor asked to be directed to the nearest hotel so he could stay for a few days. Since Sadie was refilling their coffee mugs, which she had done regularly throughout their entire visit so that she could listen in, she overheard the question.

"Honey, we don't have a hotel here in Willow Springs." She and Ben chuckled a bit at the thought of having a hotel in a town that got zero visitors per year. "No one really visits here that doesn't already have relatives living here to stay with. It isn't exactly Disney World."

The professor did not laugh at her joke. He was beginning to panic at the thought of having to navigate down that awful road in the dark.

"Tell ya what, though, sweety," Sadie continued. "I have a small room in the back that you can flop in for a few days, if you ain't too particular. It is just a cot and small bathroom. It isn't fancy, but it is free."

He was very grateful for her hospitality. He usually was very particular about where he stayed, but right now he would have slept in a dumpster if it meant that he did not have to drive back down to the city tonight. "You are most gracious. I very much appreciate your hospitality." So, Sadie took Professor Morningstar to the tiny room so he could get settled for the evening, and they agreed that he could meet Xuan in the morning.

Ben returned to the house, thinking how nice it was to have another outsider in town. He and Diana were still planning to leave in a few days, but until then, it was nice not to be the new guy. When he got back, he found Diana once again struggling with Barley. He watched her wrestle with the giant dog for a few minutes, trying to convince him to go out into the yard for even a few moments. He could not control his laughter. "Let me help you. Come on, Barley, it is time to pee-pee."

“I just don't get what is going on with the silly dog,” she responded, not appreciating her husband’s laughter. “He loves the outside, and usually we can't get him to come in. Now he won't go out.

“Maybe it is time for you to finally admit that your dog has a mental issue,” he joked, leaning forward to kiss her. “I wouldn't worry about it. He probably saw some big, bad cricket or something that scared him. He will be fine when we get home.” Finally, the two of them were able to get the dog outside long enough to do his business, and then he zipped right past them back into the house and into his hiding corner. Diana just shook her head. *How could something so big be so scared of a little bug?* she thought. Then she put her arm around Ben as they walked back into the house together.

“My dog does not have a mental issue,” she whispered, and they both laughed. They dropped onto the couch, and Ben filled her in on his long conversation with his new friend, Professor Edward Morningstar from Philadelphia. Then they headed up to bed.

The next morning, the young couple were both up early. Diana thought that early in the morning over breakfast was the best time to get Ben to discuss his plans for the house. Time was running short, and they had to return to their lives in Lancaster in just a few days. They still had a lot of decisions to make, and she worried that Ben was getting too overwhelmed to make any commitments. There was still so much stuff to go through, and he changed the subject every time she suggested that they sell the house. She was very careful to try and push him into making some final decisions without upsetting him. She once again brought up the topic, but once again, it wasn’t long until Ben was ready to head out the door to go to his meeting and refused to discuss the subject any further.

When they arrived at the diner, Sadie was outside sweeping the porch. "Good morning, folks, your professor friend is already inside waiting on you," she greeted them warmly. After she got a response, her facial expression changed sharply. "Doctor Ben, are you sure about this?" she asked quietly, leaning toward the couple so no one else could overhear.

"Am I sure about what?" Ben responded, pretending that he didn't know what she was referring to, even though he suspected she was not happy to have another stranger in town.

"Letting that man talk to Xuan. We don't know where he is really from or what his true intentions are." She paused to read their expressions. "I mean, I am not trying to be rude or anything. It is just that Xuan is special, and we don't usually introduce her to strangers."

Ben put his arm on her shoulder and smiled. "It's alright, Sadie, I understand perfectly. Uncle Leonard seemed to think that Professor Morningstar could help Xuan, and I have to trust that he knew what he was talking about."

Sadie took a deep breath. She greatly admired Doc Bashore and had to agree with Ben that if this was his idea, it must be the right thing to do. "Alright then, you go in and grab some breakfast, and I will go fetch Xuan." She faked a smile as she turned to put down the broom.

Diana chuckled as she entered the diner and saw the professor. With his long black hair pulled back into a low ponytail, long suede jacket, and turquoise ring, he looked exactly like she had pictured him in her head. They did the standard polite greetings, and then sat down to order their breakfast. Diana was very curious as to why this man wanted to meet a little girl. She was also hoping that perhaps he had more information about where Xuan came from and how she became the orphan of Willow Springs. The story intrigued her, and no one in town seemed comfortable discussing it. Whenever she asked a question about the little native girl, they were pretty skilled at changing the subject or creating a distraction. Perhaps Ben's uncle had uncovered more information about her origins or where her parents were, or why they dressed her in animal skin dresses and not pretty little girl clothing like the rest of the kids in town. She noticed that Edward had a large envelope stuffed with papers. Perhaps the clues to this mystery were in there.

Xuan came bursting into the diner full of energy, like most six-year-olds, and climbed into the booth next to Diana. She pushed a rock that she had been carrying over to her new friend and smiled brightly. Diana picked it up and examined it.

"Whoa, Xuan, that is a great rock. You found a really pretty one. Good job."

The little girl was proud that her friend liked her treasure. Professor Morningstar introduced himself to the girl and tried to warm up to her. She seemed to like him very quickly and was not afraid. He asked her many questions. She listened intently, like she was interested in the conversation, but she simply did not speak. He spoke to her in the Iroquois language and asked if she understood. She nodded but still did not speak. He continued to talk. Diana did not understand what was being said, but she did know that the little girl was not uncomfortable and wanted to participate. She flipped the placemat over and slid the blank side to Xuan. She reached to the back of the table and picked up a crayon. Xuan got busy drawing two large figures and one small one that appeared to be people. Both adults understood that it was her family. She then drew a large circle around her mother's midsection. Diana sadly looked at Edward as he asked

Xuan if that was her mother. The little girl nodded and got busy drawing again.

Diana quietly mouthed the words, "Her mother was pregnant when she died." He sadly nodded back.

Xuan drew a large furry head with big teeth and big eyes. She pushed very hard on the crayon and zig-zagged around the face, repeatedly drawing fur.

The professor pointed to the face and asked the little girl who was it that she was drawing now.

The little girl answered with the first word anyone had heard her speak in a very long time: "Yona."

CHAPTER NINE

SILAS BARNETT'S SON COLLIN grew up to be as arrogant and self-centered as his father. After all, why wouldn't he? He was given everything he needed in life without having to do any work. His father constantly reminded him that they were better than most of the people he would meet and they deserved to take everything they wanted, no matter the affect it had on anyone else. His mother spent all her time trying to please her husband and climb the social ladder as high as she could. She was always planning the perfect party, supporting the right charity, or campaigning for the right candidate. She focused her time on whatever would gain her the most notoriety. She and her husband competed to see who could be in the paper or on the news the most times each year. She loved her son greatly, but staying home with him would not bolster her standing in the community much—and after all, she'd paid a professional nanny to mind Collin. What more could she do for him, really?

Collin hated college. He didn't like the professors acting like they knew more than he did, and all he wanted to do was to quit school and work with his father. Why did he need an education for that? His dad was the best. He could learn all he needed to know from him. His parents did not agree and had big plans for his graduation, so they needed him to finish his schooling. Now in his second year, he spent most of his time in the basement of their mansion, getting drunk with his three best friends. It was not easy hanging out with Collin—he could be a real jerk and was quite often downright mean—but he had a lot of money, and all the cool gadgets and toys. His friends knew that Collin's father was connected to all the powerful people if they ever needed any help, so they put up with Collin's awful personality and pretended to enjoy hanging out with him.

The four friends were lounging in the basement once again, getting drunk and playing video games. Collin's best friend, Andrew, saw some blueprints spread out on a table in a corner. He shuffled through them and found a map of the wooded mountain north of Wilkes-Barre.

"Dude, what is all this stuff? I recognize this area. We went hunting up there a few years ago."

Collin rolled his eyes at the thought of getting off his comfortable chair and walking over to the table. "That's my dad's stuff. Some stupid project he dreams of building, says it will triple his money." He joined his friend at the table and riffled through the pile of papers, pulling out another map. "This mountain is filled with natural hot springs. He wants to build a resort up there. He is sure all of the world's richest people will flood into town to enjoy the mystical powers of these amazing mud puddles."

The boys all laughed. "Well, your dad has done pretty good so far. He is probably onto something there. When does he break ground?" Andrew asked.

Collin took another gulp of his beer and shook his head. "He can't yet. There is some Godforsaken town right in the middle of it, and those slugs don't want to move." He picked up a fistful of darts and started hurling them at a dart board on the wall behind Andrew's head. "The town is ridiculously small, only about two hundred old houses. It's been there since the beginning of time and they won't sell. They cry that their families have been there forever, and they don't want to go anywhere else." Collin said in a whiny voice, pretending to wipe a tear from his eye.

"Your dad will get them to sell. He always finds a way to get what he wants," another boy called out, still glued to the television screen, trying not to interrupt his video game.

Collin hurled another dart. "I don't know about that. He is trying to negotiate with them and is going to court to try and find a way to force them out. I say we kill them all and bury them in the woods where no one will find them." Then he took the last dart and slammed it into the map, straight through the town of Willow Springs and deep into the wood table. As he turned to return to his chair, a thought hit him like a brick. *His father wanted that land more than anything. If he could get the townspeople to give it up, his dad would have to let him drop out of school and join his company.*

'Do you know what?" he asked his friends. "It's time for those people to come into this century and move down into the city. They need to get out of the way of modern progress. They have it too easy. Come on, we are going to give them a wakeup call." He grabbed his jacket and headed for the door.

Andrew was worried about what his friend was planning. "Dude, wait, what?"

"We are going to harass the town until they decide to move."

"Nah, come on, let's just go find some girls," Andrew suggested.

The kid playing video games was so drunk, he didn't want to move. "No, guys, why don't we just crash here? This is fine, right? I will buy some pizzas, call it in."

Collin wouldn't hear of it. His mind was made up; they were going. He gave them the look that they all knew meant he was getting his way or they would be cut off, so they grumbled and agreed.

Great, Andrew thought to himself as he shut off the light and locked the basement door. *We are going to harass a bunch of farmers, and I am going to get arrested, woohoo!*

It was about 7:00 at night when the guys finally made it up the road to Willow Springs, and most of the townspeople were at the church. They immediately made their way into the diner and started harassing the young waitress who was on duty. An older gentleman stood up to assist her, but Collin shoved the man, and he fell into a booth.

"Dude, do you really want to hurt someone?" one of the kids ask their friend.

"Shut up," Collin snarled back. He was on a mission.

The waitress didn't want the man to get hurt, so she smiled and told him she would be fine. Then she suggested that he go to the church to get the mayor. Collin began throwing dishes and knocking over tables throughout the diner, warning that they should close it down and move out of town. Two of the boys joined in the destruction, but Andrew stood in shock. He was a good kid who was in over his head. "Collin, they went to get the mayor. Let's just go," he pleaded.

Collin laughed. "It's cool, dude, you can take the ninety-year-old mayor." Then he ran outside, picked up a rock, and threw it through a glass window across the way. Andrew's heart sank. He didn't want any part of this but couldn't get out of it, so he headed back to the car hoping Collin didn't see him leave and get mad. Collin and the other two boys were moving fast now—breaking windows, throwing stuff around, and knocking over anything in their path. The more destruction they caused, the higher their adrenaline rush soared.

Andrew crouched down in the passenger seat of Collin's convertible, hoping his friends would just come back to the car so they could leave. It seemed like they were taking forever. The longer he waited, the more impatient he became. Suddenly, he noticed movement out of the corner of his eye. He turned his head to look behind him and squinted hard to see through the dark. He thought he saw an animal or something duck behind the support column on a nearby porch. He opened the car door and swung his legs out, turning his body to get a better look. He was really scared now. Xuan's tiny face peeped out around the pole. Relieved, he released the breath he was holding and smiled for a moment. It was just a little girl, not a vicious animal or an angry townsperson coming to beat him up for what Collin was doing. Then he heard his friend's chaos getting closer, and his relief turned to fear again.

"Little girl, you have to go hide," he whispered to Xuan. "Go, go hide." He motioned with his hands to try and shoo her away. She was confused. He put his hands over his face and repeated "You have to run and hide. Stay away from those bad guys."

Xuan seemed to understand him and ran behind the car to duck down behind some trash cans. Just then, the people began filing out of the church to see what the commotion was all about. Collin and the other two boys came running to the car excitedly, laughing. They were pumped up and pretty proud of the chaos that they were causing. Collin immediately started the car to try and leave as people started throwing things at the car to try and stop them.

"Where were you, ya dick?" he said to Andrew as he ducked to avoid a bottle that flew past his head and hit the dashboard of the car. Collin laughed heartily. Andrew had never seen him so happy. "Time to go!" Collin put the car into reverse and slammed the gas pedal to the floor. The tires spun, squealed, and kicked up dirt and thick smoke. The car shot backwards and slammed into the trash cans, throwing Xuan's tiny body violently onto the porch.

Andrew panicked and grabbed the driver's arm. "Collin, stop!" he yelled. "The little girl, I think you killed her." He looked at his friend and was shocked to see no empathy or regret in his eyes at all. He was almost smiling. Andrew pulled his hand away, as if he were trying to get away from a monster. Collin shifted the car and floored the gas pedal again, speeding down the road and out of town.

No one in the car said a word as they sped down the windy road, bumping through the potholes and skidding around the turns. After several long moments, Collin broke the silence. "What is with you guys?" he yelled suddenly. "That's the most fun we had in months. Did you see those mooks chasing us? It was funny as hell."

The friends were in shock. "Are you freaking kidding me, Collin?" a boy in the back seat screamed, grabbing hold of the seat to pull himself forward. "Did you miss the part where we killed a kid, Collin? Did you miss that? Even your father can't fix this." He slammed back into the seat and dropped his head into his hands.

The other boy in the back chimed in, "We are going to jail. I can't do jail."

Collin couldn't believe his friends were so down and spoiling his fun. “Assholes, no one is going to jail. That kid will be fine. Stop being buzzkills and hand me a beer.” Collin turned around to reach into the back seat to grab a bottle when all of a sudden, a large black animal crossed into the road. All three of the other boys shouted at the same time: “Collin!” He spun around just before hitting the animal. He swung the wheel hard to the right, and the car slid out of control and down the embankment on the side of the road, slamming head-on into the rocks below. The crash was deafening. The front end of the car exploded into a barrage of flying parts. Then there was nothing but silence.

CHAPTER TEN

AS THE SUN ROSE OVER the Barnett mansion, Collin's mother realized that he had not returned home the night before. This was not too terribly odd, being that he was in college, but as the day went on and he had not turned up to eat or ask for money, her concern grew by the hour. His cell phone was going directly to voicemail, so she questioned the staff to see if they knew where he was headed or what his plans were. When that provided no useful information, she reached out to all the parents of his friends whom she was familiar with. When she discovered that several boys had not returned home in almost an entire day, she went into her husband's den.

"Silas, I can't find Collin," she began to say.

He cut her off without even looking up from the computer. "He is not in here. Shut the door when you leave, please."

She began again. "Silas, I called everyone. No one has seen him since last night, and his phone is shut off. Something is wrong." She moved closer to get his attention. "Silas, a mother knows when something is wrong."

Annoyed that he had to interrupt a work project to appease her, he flopped back in his chair and sighed loudly. When he finally looked up to see the distress on her face, he rose to hug her tightly.

"Alright, let's go find your son." He put his hand on her back to lead her out of the office toward the living room. "And then we will kill him for worrying his mother." His wife did not find that funny.

For hours, the couple continued to make phone calls, but no one that they spoke to had any information on the whereabouts of their son. When Silas ran out of other ideas, he called his friends at the police station. Now, normally a person has to be missing for a minimum of forty-eight hours before an official report can be filed, but things move a little faster when a Barnett is missing. Within hours, the house was filled with investigators and news media. Mrs. Barnett invited the parents of the other missing boys over to the house to wait with her for information. This was not done out of sympathy or concern. She just figured it would make a bigger news story and get more coverage.

For the next two days, the news coverage was non-stop. Silas and his wife sat on the couch, anxiously waiting for their son to be found. They cried and prayed with the other parents—in front of the cameras, of course—and it was the biggest news story in the Wilkes-Barre valley. The couple's friends sent a stream of flowers and gifts of support, and the phone rang endlessly with well-wishers. It was an exhausting nightmare to sit hour after hour and not know where their son was. Silas still suspected that his son would come staggering in the door after some wild adventure, and everything would be right again. His wife Suzanne knew in her heart that the situation would most likely have a different outcome. No matter what her son did, he always checked in with his mother each morning. She knew something seriously wrong was preventing him from checking in.

Silas grew tired of sitting and waiting. He decided that he would go out and try to find his son. Just as he stood to leave his wife's side, his assistant poked her head in the doorway. “Mr. Barnett, there is a Detective Yeagar at the door for you.”

“Thank you, Colleen.” Suzanne jumped up to follow her husband to the door, but he told her stay with their guests. “It probably isn't anything new, just more questions.” He patted his wife’s hand and went to the door. The detective tried his best to be sensitive while he informed the man that they had located Collin's car and that there had been a terrible accident. Silas's face went blank, and he was unable to hear anything that the detective said after that. He leaned on the door frame, trying desperately to get any air at all into his lungs. He felt as though he were being crushed. His heart was pounding as if it was about to burst from his chest. Detective Yeagar put his hand on Silas's elbow to support him in case he passed out.

“Mr. Barnett, are you alright?” he asked several times. “Mr. Barnett?”

Silas turned suddenly to his assistant, Colleen, who was sneaking up behind him, for support. He knew that he should go back in to his wife to help her through receiving the news, but all he could think of was that he had to get away from all these people. He looked his assistant in the eye and muttered, “Colleen, tell Suzanne her son is dead.” Then he pushed past the detective and out the door.

By the time Silas arrived at his son's accident scene, the sun was setting and the flashing lights of the emergency vehicles were blinding. He sat in the car for a moment. *They have to be wrong*, he thought, *it can't be Collin. There is no way he would be on this awful road. It can't be him.* A state police trooper saw his car pull up and headed over to greet him.

Silas opened the car door to get out, but the trooper blocked him. "You can't be here, sir, it is an active emergency scene."

Silas could barely speak. Looking up at the officer for the first time, he pleaded, "It is my son." The trooper could see the sadness in the father's eyes. It was not the first time in his career that he had experienced the grief of family members before. He leaned down in empathy.

"I know, sir, but you can't go down there. There is nothing you can do here." He put his hand on Mr. Barnett's shoulder for comfort. "Go home to your wife, she needs you now. You have arrangements to make." Silas nodded in agreement and could feel tears welling in his eyes. He reached for the door handle, and the officer backed out of the way. As the car backed out to leave, the trooper headed down the embankment to the accident scene. It was dark and the brush was thick, so he had to be careful making his way. He knew the coroner was examining the bodies, so he called out to him to confirm he was going in the right direction. "What are we looking at, Doc?"

"Not sure about the cause of the accident yet, but I know these poor guys are looking at a closed-casket funeral," the doctor's voice replied from a few feet away. As the trooper finally pushed through the brush to where he could see the car, he stopped dead in his tracks. Although he had worked hundreds of accident investigations in his career, this was by far the most gruesome thing that he had ever witnessed.

The car was stuck fast to the rock in front of it, and the four boys were sitting straight up in their seats, without their heads. He blinked his eyes quickly to make sure it was real and not an illusion. The coroner, Bill Singer, was leaning over the driver's side door, taking measurements of the wounds. There was a fireman at the edge of the bushes, vomiting. Dr. Singer looked up at the officer "Welcome."

Still trying to comprehend the horror he was looking at, all he could mutter back was, "Doc, what the hell?"

The doc stood up and walked around the car with his camera. "This isn't the first time that we have seen decapitation in auto accidents involving convertibles," he reminded the trooper. He turned to look at the doctor as he came around the back of the vehicle. This helped to snap him back into the moment a bit.

"That's true, usually when the car slides under a large truck. Do you think a truck was involved and left the scene?" He turned his eyes back to the car. He just could not look away. *Why are they still sitting up*? He noticed that Collin's hands were still on the steering wheel, as if he were still driving. It was beyond eerie.

Another officer walked over, shaking his head, and chimed into the conversation. "The skid marks on the road indicate that the convertible swerved to avoid something in the road and crashed down the embankment. There isn't a second set of skid marks, so it is unlikely that there was another vehicle involved. There is alcohol on scene, so either some sort of animal ran in front of them, or the driver was just too drunk to navigate the winding road."

The first trooper turned to his colleague. "Okay, so then where are their heads?"

"That I don't know, but now that you are here, it's all yours to figure out." He tore out a page of notes from his notebook and handed it to the other officer, and then headed back up the embankment to his car.

The doctor held his camera up to the trooper and flipped through a few pictures for him. "I think I have that answer. Do you see those deep gouges along the neck?" The officer felt his stomach churn. He was trying not to vomit, so he just nodded without speaking. "They are tooth impressions"

"So, you believe that animals ate their heads?" Now the trooper was waiting to wake up. He was sure this had to be a bad dream.

"Most likely one animal." He flipped to another photo and zoomed in on it. "It appears that the heads were removed with a single bite."

The trooper was more confused than ever. "So, you are telling me that a Tyrannosaurus rex killed these kids? Doc, I don't have time for this." The doctor shook his head. "Then what could make a bite mark that large?" He was getting annoyed.

Still shaking his head, the doctor didn't have much more information than that. "I don't know, a bear maybe, but it would have to be about twenty feet tall. Or maybe a shark, a whale—or yeah, a Tyrannosaurus rex." Both men stood silent for a moment. "Look, I don't know. I got to get these guys back to the morgue to know for sure, but this is what I got out here in the field. It is definitely bite marks."

The trooper patted his shoulder. "Alright, Doc, do your thing, and I will circle back to you when you know more." The officers combed the scene and surrounding woods throughout the entire night, looking for evidence of what caused the accident and what animal could have possibly been involved. They found no footprints or fur of any kind.

When Silas returned home, the police officers had left, but the home was still full of reporters and well-wishers. He could not bring himself to face them right away, so he sat in his car and began to cry. He had lost his only son. He was not used to losing anything. It took quite a long time for him to pull himself together enough to even get out of the car. Once his loss and sorrow started to make the ugly turn to anger, he slammed into the house and yelled for everyone to get out. His wife had been sedated and had passed out in her grief, so Silas headed downstairs to the basement that Collin spent most of his time in. Several of his closest friends ignored his commands to leave and followed him to attempt to console their boss.

On the way down to the basement Silas grabbed a bottle out of the kitchen and threw the cap across the room, planning to drink it all. He needed to ease his pain any way he could. He drank and cried and went through his son's belongings, desperately looking for something that would make him feel closer to Collin. The men in the room felt for the grieving father and could not imagine his pain, but had no idea what to say to help. They sat quietly for a few hours and allowed him to express his grief.

The more that he drank and the later it got, the more his sadness turned to anger and guilt. He thought of all the things he could have done to prevent the accident. He could have paid more attention to what his son was doing. He could have had rules and discipline that prevented drinking and driving. He could have taught his son better behavior, but he did not want to think about that. He could not bear the weight of the guilt, so he desperately wanted to find someone else to blame for the loss of his boy. It had to be someone else's fault. Perhaps somebody else was driving, or someone cut them off. He walked over to the table where the project blueprints were still spread across the table. He saw the dart driven through the dot that marked Willow Springs. He pulled it out and lifted the map to get a closer look. At that moment, he realized why Collin's car was on that awful road. His son had gone up to the town. He was trying to help with the project.

“Those back-ass people did this,” he muttered.

Not understanding his thoughts, his friend Jack ask him to repeat it.

"They killed my boy!" Silas snapped. "And damn it, they have to pay." He slammed the paper back on the table and headed upstairs to his car. His friends were confused and looked at each other, shrugging. They were tired and wanted to leave, but you didn't upset Silas, so they trudged up after him.

"Silas, where are you going? You need to get some sleep," Jack pleaded.

"Fuck sleep. Somebody has to pay for this. I'm going to that Godforsaken town, and somebody is going to tell me who killed my son!" He went to the garage, gathered up several short pieces of lumber, and threw them into his car trunk, then sped off into the night. His friends were very nervous about what they were about to get into but knew that they could not leave the drunk, grieving man alone right now. They jumped into a pickup and quickly followed him, hoping to stop him from whatever he was planning to do.

CHAPTER ELEVEN

DIANA CRIED UNCONTROLLABLY as she watched Ben and Edward lift Xuan's lifeless body. "Please God, let her be alright," she prayed through her tears. Ben ran to his office to gather supplies as Edward took the girl into the church. The crowd stepped back to make a path for him to pass. He laid her gently at the front of the altar and brushed her long black hair away from her face. Ben slid up beside him and wildly began yanking tools out of a huge bag, trying to save her. He barked orders at Edward and handed him a syringe.

"My friend, I am not a nurse," he protested.

Ben looked up for a brief moment. "You are tonight. I will do whatever I can with my medicine, and you will work your magic with yours. Together, we have to save Xuan." Both men nodded and continued to work on the tiny girl. Ben continued to do CPR, and Edward chanted an ancient native prayer asking the spirit guides to help the little girl. The entire town watched and prayed and comforted each other. Sadie put her arm around Diana.

"If anyone can save that little girl, it is your man. I know he is a good doctor," she reassured her new friend.

As the night went on, the townspeople went home to bed, still praying for poor Xuan. One by one they realized that they were of no help staying at the church and disappeared into the night to return to their homes. As the sun began to peep over the mountain in the very early moments of morning, Ben touched Diana's cheek as she slept on a church pew. She gasped and shot up awake.

"Let's go get some sleep," he whispered.

Trying to peek past him to see the little girl, she asked, "Is she..." but she couldn't even finish the question for fear of the answer.

"She is stable for now. Edward and Berta are going to take turns staying with her. We can get some rest for a few hours, and then see about transferring her to the city hospital." Diana nodded and followed her husband, although she suspected that there was no way anyone in this town was going to let their little Xuan go down to the city.

After a few hours of sleep, Ben was still exhausted but needed to go check on his patient at the church. He was determined that he needed to move the girl down to the city hospital for further treatment. As he poured a cup of coffee in the kitchen to try and get some energy, Diana came up behind him, wrapping her arms around his waist to lay her head on his back. "Do you think she will make it?" she asked, knowing that he did not really have any way to predict an outcome and would be pushing hard to transport the girl.

Ben swung around to face her so he could hug her back. "Not if I don't get her to a real hospital soon." Just then, there was a knock on the door. The couple looked at each other in concern, hoping that it was not bad news about their patient. Ben opened the door slowly to find Professor Morningstar, Sadie, and Ned Ferguson standing together, holding a box of papers.

Sadie spoke first in her motherly tone. "I know you didn't get much rest, but could we come in for a while? We need to talk about Xuan." She smiled at him.

Ben's heart sank, "Did we..." he paused. "Did we lose her?"

"No, no, no. She is still stable but unconscious. Berta is with her and will let us know if she needs anything," the professor reassured him. "We just have to make some long-term decisions for her." Ben was hopeful that they were all on the same page and ready to move the girl to a hospital. He showed them in, and they all sat in the living room. Diana offered them coffee, but everyone was anxious to get deep into conversation, so they declined.

Sadie explained to the couple that the town understood why Ben wanted to move the girl, but they simply could not allow her to leave Willow Springs for any reason. Ben implored them that her head injury was serious and he could not care for her effectively with the tools he had at his access now. They went back and forth for almost an hour, and it was becoming obvious that they would not agree.

Sadie finally blurted out quite loudly, "She won't die, no matter what!"

Edward stood up. He reached into his shirt to remove a long chain that he wore around his neck. On the end of the chain was a large gold key. He handed it to Sadie. "Do you know where the drawer is?" he asked. She nodded and led him into Ben's uncle's office. Ben and Diana followed after them and watched in shock as Sadie opened the drawer in the middle of the wall. She stepped back to allow Edward access to the drawer. He slowly reached in and pulled out a thick file, and then apologized to Ben. "We have not been completely honest with you about Xuan, I am afraid." Seeing that Diana was a bit irked that he had the key that she'd spent hours looking for all this time, he felt he had to acknowledge her. "Ben's uncle sent me a copy of the key so that I could continue his work, if anything happened to him."

"What work?" Ben asked.

"He was trying to free Xuan from an ancient spell." Edward waited for a reaction from the couple after he said this. He himself still wasn't sure that he believed it, so he really didn't expect anyone else to believe it either. But the couple was more interested in what was in the folder than what the professor was saying, so they didn't react much as he continued. He opened the file onto the desk and explained to them the story of how Xuan's tribe had been annihilated, and her mother had tried to bless her with protection, but something went wrong. They talked about how the little girl ended up in the town of Willow Springs, and flipped through documents trailing the families that had taken care of her and passed her down from generation to generation, almost as if she were a precious heirloom. As she slowly flipped through the book that Sarah had made a very long time ago, Diana somehow knew that this story was true, even though it defied the laws of nature as we know them. Ben, however, was not even close to convinced. In fact, he was shocked that his intelligent, educated new friend was even saying such things.

"Edward, stop. You don't seriously believe that we have a three-hundred-year-old little girl living here, do you?" he asked, laughing slightly. The adults stood silent for a moment. "I mean, come on. That's not even possible."

Edward spoke slowly, trying to choose his words carefully. "I don't want to believe it, trust me. All my life, I have been taught about the special powers that my people are supposed to have and the spirits that guide and protect us. I am supposed to believe in them, but I struggle with the logic of it, just as many of you struggle with your religious faith. But your uncle, Ben, he was sure of it. Look at his evidence, and then decide for yourself."

So, Ben flipped through the file and was more drawn to his uncle's notes than the antique pictures that showed the same little girl wearing the same color dress, over and over again.

Sadie pulled a picture out of her bag and looked at Ned for a moment. He nodded his head, as if to give her permission to show the young couple. She slid the picture to Diana first. "This is me as a child." Diana picked up the black-and-white photo to see a small, light-haired girl that was obviously Sadie standing next to Xuan. They were the same size. "I played with Xuan when I was a child; we all did. She was my best playmate. That is why we protect her like we do. So, you see now? She can't go to General Hospital. They can't do tests on her." Sadie stopped pleading to wipe a tear from her cheek. Ben looked up from the notes to find the professor's eyes. "He thought he could cure her."

Edward nodded. "That is why he contacted me, and many other Native American shamans. He was looking for the words to reverse whatever spell her mother used, so that she could grow up as a normal girl and eventually die."

Ned leaned toward Ben. "So, you see, her injuries may be serious, but she won't die. She hasn't for almost three hundred years." Ben and Diana looked at each other, not knowing what to say. Edward continued to fill them in on what Uncle Leonard had come across in his thirty years of research, and what the collective shamans had tried so far.

Ben continued to flip through the notebook. "What is Yona?" he asked. When no one answered him, he pointed to a passage in the notebook and turned it so they could all see it. "It says 'Beware of Yona.' What is Yona?"

"The word means *Great Bear*," Edward explained. "My people believe that we all have a spiritual animal guide that leads and protects us. Xuan's seems to be a bear."

The pieces of the puzzle started coming together for Diana, and she blurted out, "Oh my God, it's true." Ben just looked at her, waiting for more of an explanation. "It's true, she has a spiritual guide. It's a bear. It makes sense now."

Ben thought she was either being sarcastic or making a joke and worried that she was about to offend his guests, but she was serious. She jumped to her feet and started pacing nervously.

"It makes perfect sense now," she continued. "Henry tried to hurt Xuan behind the market, and I told him that if he touched her again, he would lose his hand, and he did. Something in the woods took off his hand. It was a bear." She stopped pacing and turned toward the others, who all still looked a bit confused. "It was her bear protector, it had to be. And then when Barley knocked her over, you were worried about him." She pointed to Sadie. "You were worried that her protector was going to get Barley. That is why he is suddenly afraid of the outside."

Ben interrupted her. "Honey, you are rambling. Don't you think that we are all getting a little carried away with this?" But no one else in the room agreed. "Alright then, so you are saying that we have a three-hundred-year-old Native American girl who cannot die, and she has a spiritual bear that protects her?" He paused, waiting for someone to laugh. No one did, so he began to give in to their argument. "What do we do now?"

"You have to stay in Willow Springs for a while longer," Ned suggested.

Before Ben could resist the idea, Edward continued, "You need to take care of her until she recovers, and then we will work together to figure out how to break the spell."

Much to everyone's surprise, Ben did not argue. He could see from the look on his wife's face that returning to Lancaster had become the farthest thing from her mind over the past few days. He agreed to think about it. He still was not convinced of the story they'd told, but he did understand that the little girl needed to be cared for, and she wasn't going to the hospital anytime soon.

Feeling as though they had achieved their initial mission, the trio departed to allow the couple to digest the new information that had been dropped upon them. Ben and Diana sat for a while sorting through the pile of pictures. "Wow," Diana sighed as she flopped back into her chair. "I knew this town was secluded, but who knew they could possibly have such secrets?"

"Yeah, I hear you. Let's just hope there are not too many more secrets that we don't know about yet." He reached over and patted her knee as he stood up. "Well, I have to go check on Xuan. Can you start making some phone calls to see if we can stay here for a little while without losing our apartment and jobs and friends and shirts?" he continued to mutter as he walked out of the room.

"Ben," she yelled to him. As he poked his head back around the door frame, she kissed him on the forehead and smiled. "Everything really is going to be alright."

CHAPTER TWELVE

BACK AT SILAS'S MANSION, the men left the house and headed into the city. They followed their boss, hoping to find a way to talk him out of doing anything rash. When he turned in at one of his construction sites, they were relieved. Apparently, he was planning to bury his sorrow with work, and soon they would be able to head home.

Silas staggered out of his vehicle and went to unlock the gate that surrounded the work site. He could barely stand and had to hold himself up by grasping the chain link fencing with one hand as he fumbled with the lock with the other. When he dropped the large set of keys on the ground, his foreman, Grady, ran to pick them up. Angry at the notion that someone actually had the nerve to suggest he needed help, Silas shoved him away hard and yelled, "I can do it." He bent down to get the keys and stumbled toward the ground. Grady caught him and leaned him up against the gate.

"Boss, let me take you home," he pleaded.

Silas swatted his hand at him and made a snarling sound. Nothing was going to dissuade him from his mission. He grabbed the keys, opened the lock, pushed open the gate, and started bumbling around the construction site gathering supplies. The men were tired and wanted to go home. They knew they couldn't leave their boss alone, or he would get in serious trouble. They were trained to do whatever Silas wanted, whenever he wanted, and usually get yelled at in the end anyway. They needed the job and enjoyed the perks that came from hanging around with Silas Barnett. The men looked at one another to see if anyone knew exactly what they were up to. Grady just shrugged and followed his boss. Silas tore through crates and boxes, grabbing items and shoving them into the arms of his gang, who piled them into the pickup truck trying to figure out what the agenda was. When Silas unlocked the explosives cabinet, the men knew they were in way over their heads. Grady tried to push the cabinet door back shut. "Boss, let's slow down and think for a minute. What exactly are you planning to do? This stuff can't leave the site, or we could get arrested." His tone turned desperate. "We aren't licensed to remove explosives."

Silas pushed him aside and snarled once again. He was Silas Barnett, he absolutely could not imagine ever being held accountable for anything he did. There was always a way out, always someone to bail him out of trouble.

The men quickly hatched a plan to distract their boss from his vengeful mission. They convinced him to go into the trailer they used for an office and pulled out a bottle. Perhaps if they could get him to drink just a little bit more, he would pass out, and they could sneak away with no punishment. So for the next few hours they took turns refilling his glass and desperately trying to get him to talk about his business, his buildings, new projects he was considering—anything other than the loss of his only son.

As the hours ticked by, their exhaustion grew, but they were sure the plan was working. Any minute the boss would drift off, and they could all go home. No such luck came their way. Late in the afternoon, Silas jumped to his feet, staggered out to the trucks, and demanded to be driven up the mountain to Willow Springs. The gang complied with his wishes, as usual, and piled into the vehicles and headed out of town to the winding road that led to Willow Springs.

Grady was driving slowly, still hoping the ride would put Silas to sleep. The trucks bounced back and forth as the tires worked their way through the deep crevasses in the broken blacktop. Even though it was still daylight, the forest was very dark. The trees were so thick that the space between them appeared dark as night. You could not see more than two feet off either side of the road. *Geez, anything could be in there,* Grady thought to himself. He had never realized how creepy the wilderness could be. He spent most of his time in the city, surrounded by people and buildings. As he slowly maneuvered around a hard bend, he was sure he saw something dark run into the trees on the left. While he was searching the tree line on the left, a large rock came bouncing down the right side and shot out from between the trees, heading straight for the truck.

"Look out!" screamed the voices from the back seat. He spun the wheel hard, but it was too late. The rock slammed into the front wheel, throwing the truck out of control. It swerved back and forth before bouncing off the side of the road and into the ditch. The second truck slammed on the brakes and skidded to a stop right behind the first. The guys jumped out and ran down into the ditch to help. No one was injured, but the front axle and wheel were completely destroyed. After the guys pulled themselves together, Grady got out his cell phone, his hands still shaking, and began to wander around the side of the road attempting to find a signal.

"What are you doing?" Silas yelled at him. "Put that damn thing away and get this stuff into the other truck."

"I'm trying to get a tow truck to pick us up," he explained.

"A tow truck? What the fuck for? We will put everything into that truck and leave this one right here. Let's go," Silas snapped as he slammed the tailgate down and started throwing the supplies at his team. They were in absolute shock that not even an accident was going to stop this guy and turn him back. Once again, they gave in to his wishes, loaded up the second truck, and jumped into the back to continue on up the winding road. When they were just south of the town, Silas ordered them to turn off onto a tiny path that was almost too small to fit the pickup. The guys in the back almost fell out as the truck shook violently, trying to negotiate through the tight forest.

"Take it easy," one of them shouted. "Are you trying to kill us?"

"I'm doing the best I can. Do you want to drive?" the driver snapped.

Finally, Silas gave the word that they could stop and get out. He hurried to grab some gas cans and disappeared into the trees. The driver turned to Grady as if he knew what was going on. "He isn't going to try and burn those folks out of their homes, is he?" Grady shrugged but was pretty sure he knew that was exactly what his boss was doing. "You do realize that with this wind, if he does start a forest fire, we could be trapped in it too?" Grady turned to walk away, but the driver grabbed his shoulder and turned him back. "What if something happens to this truck? What if we can't get out? What if we get caught?" All the men were beginning to panic.

"What do you want to do, leave him out here?" He spun around to all the men, searching each of their faces for an answer. "Seriously, what are our choices right now, guys? 'Cause I am open to suggestions." With nothing but silence returned as an answer, he turned and headed into the brush to find his boss.

The plan was to start a line of fire just above the town, hoping the warm summer wind would push it into town and force the people of Willow Springs to evacuate and abandon their homes. If the town were destroyed, then maybe they would finally be willing to sell their property. Silas staggered around the trees, dousing them with gasoline and planning his grand forest fire. Once he lit it, they all ran back to the truck and backed slowly away. The fire started out slowly at first, but grew quickly as the dried-out timber began to catch. Flames burst up as high as the trees, and the men could feel the heat on their faces, so they backed away further. When they reached the main road once again, the truck shook with a loud rumbling sound. It almost sounded like a deep growl. They waited for a moment, looking in all directions. Then they heard another rumble, this time louder and much closer, followed by a bright flash of lightening. It was thunder. Suddenly the sky opened up and thick sheets of rain poured down. The men sat in the truck in disbelief. The ones in the back huddled down into the bed, trying to cover themselves with a small tarp. *Could this day possibly get any more miserable?* Behind them, thick smoke and steam poured up out of the trees as the heavy rain smothered the fire completely. Silas was furious. He pounded his fist on the dashboard and screamed. Grady couldn't make out exactly what he was saying. He heard a lot of cursing, something about the people up here being protected by witch doctors, and the fact that now they were headed straight into the town to scare the residents out of their homes. Sheets of rain cascaded down the windshield, making it impossible to see anything. The longer they waited for it to let up, the angrier Silas became. Luckily, the rolling thunder helped to drown out the sound of his ranting. As soon as the rain let up enough to see, the driver backed the truck around and headed for Willow Springs.

It was only a few more miles, but the dusty road had turned into a muddy mess. By the time they pulled into town, they were surprised to find that everything in town was completely dry. There hadn't been any rain there.

Silas jumped out of the truck and staggered into the center of the street. Grady and Jack followed him loyally. The others started to get out of the truck, but when Silas pulled a pistol out of the back of his pants and fired it into the air, they changed their mind and decided to wait in the vehicle, hoping this would be over quickly and they could go back home. Silas began shouting incoherently that the townspeople should gather their belongings and leave.

People began to float out of their houses to see what was going on. At first, they thought the noise was just thunder from the storm that was rolling in, but then they realized that someone was shouting. Ben and Edward told Diana to go into the diner as they checked the situation outside. She was greeted by Sadie at the door, and both women slid behind a porch post to spy on the situation. Berta tucked the blankets around Xuan and headed out of the church. She turned the light down and locked the door behind her. She wasn't sure what the ruckus was, but if there were strangers in town, she did not want them to find their little native girl. Silas continued to yell out, blaming the town for killing his boy and demanding that they surrender their property to him. Since no one appeared to be responding to him, he started randomly shooting through the windows of nearby homes and buildings.

Ben grabbed Diana, and they crouched down behind a porch post. Edward and Sadie ducked behind a parked truck. Ben prayed out loud, "Oh Lord, please don't let those bullets hit anyone." His hands shook violently as he hugged his wife tighter. The storm was moving in very quickly. The thunder was getting louder, and with each flash of lightning, they could see the thick, black, ominous clouds that were creeping in above their town.

Mr. Ferguson came bursting out of the general store carrying a broom. "Silas Barnett, go home!" he yelled. "We don't want any trouble here." The broom shook as he walked out toward Silas. "You and your guys should just leave."

Silas began to laugh. He turned toward his guys to make fun of the shop owner. "They don't want no trouble here." The three guys laughed. Jack turned to shout to the guys in the truck but was surprised that the fog had gotten so thick, he could not make out where it was parked. It was very creepy. "They killed my boy, and they don't want no trouble?" Suddenly Silas stopped laughing and his rage took back over. He pointed the gun at the terrified man and fired, hitting him in the abdomen. His men gasped in shock. Several townsfolk cried out as the poor man dropped the broom and fell backwards into the dirt.

Ben jumped to his feet and ran to the shop owner's aid. He pulled off his outer shirt, crumbled it into a ball, and pressed it hard onto the wound. Diana reached for him as he took off and tried to stop him, fearing for his safety. "Ben, no please!" Edward understood why Ben had to go help the injured man and placed his hands on Diana's shoulders to keep her from following her husband out into the open. He tried to comfort her.

Silas aimed the gun at Ben. Both men stared into each other's eyes for what seemed to be a long time. Suddenly there was a loud roll of thunder that sounded like it was right above them, followed by a horrible squealing sound coming from the truck. It sounded as if the truck was being dragged with the brakes on. The men were screaming in terror. Jack and Grady began to run toward them to help, but stopped dead in their tracks when the grinding and squealing stopped suddenly with a deafening crash somewhere in the forest. They called out to their friends but heard nothing but silence. They looked at one another, trying to figure out what was happening, and what they should do. *Do they run into the dark forest to find their friends? Do they turn back to Silas? Do they run away? What on earth is happening here?* They stood in silence, paralyzed by their terror. They could hear Silas calling out to them, but everything was spinning and they both just stood in silence. And then they heard a loud buzzing sound coming from the church. They turned their heads to see a piercing white light emanating from the building. It was so bright that you could not look at it directly. It poured out of the windows like laser beams. Everyone stared in amazement. No one knew what was happening. They forgot about the man with the gun for a moment, and Ben used the distraction to drag his injured patient out of Silas's range.

Another terrifying roll of thunder shook all the buildings in the town. It was so loud, almost as if it had originated right next to them. Everyone ducked down to cover their ears in fear. The men moved closer to Silas. The doors of the church exploded open, and the bright light burst out into the street. Several townspeople put their hands up to shield their eyes and began to walk toward the church. A small silhouette appeared to be drifting out of the light, moving toward them. It was Xuan—she was awake and on her feet. Berta called out to her, fearing that Silas would shoot the little girl next but then she saw that Xuan's eyes were glowing with the same white light that filled the church. "What is happening?" she whispered. Tribal drums began to beat in the forest encircling the town.

"Edward, what is happening?" Sadie asked, expecting that he would have answers. "Is this some sort of magic from your people?" She could see by the blank look on his face that he either did not know what was happening, or he still did not believe, but she continued to question him anyway. "Are we in danger?" He put his arm around her and pulled her close to comfort her. It was all he had.

Silas was so terrified and drunk that he just could not process what he was doing. He raised the gun and pointed it directly at Xuan. She met his gaze and tilted her head slightly. She slowly reached her arms up toward the sky. The warm wind ruffled her dress and blew her hair. She smiled slightly, and in a deep, loud voice that was far too big to be from a little girl, shouted one word: "Yona!" Suddenly her head dropped backwards sharply, and the light from her eyes burst upward and lit up the entire night sky. The thick black clouds over the church were now in the shape of a humongous bear with large, snarling fangs and vicious claws. It was big, it was terrifying, and it was angry.

The drums from the forest were getting louder and louder. Edward Morningstar could no longer deny the magic of his people and had found the connection to his religion that he had searched for his entire life. Tears streamed down his cheeks. He dropped to his knees and began chanting a prayer to his ancestors.

Jack began to run down the road to escape. Suddenly his body flew into the air and up against a shed wall, as if some large, invisible force had smacked him very hard. When he landed at the foot of the shed, his body was ripped with claw marks. Seeing this, Grady ran the opposite direction into the woods. There was a growl, followed by a shrill scream, and then silence. Silas was terrified. He didn't understand what was going on, and now he was alone. He started shooting again, and the townspeople once again took cover. There was another brilliant flash of lightning, followed by more deafening thunder that sounded like a growl. Silas aimed his gun at the terrifying bear that was moving closer to him. He kept firing into the cloud even after he was out of bullets. His entire body shook violently with fear as Yona moved right above him, snarling. The drums kept getting louder. The town hid their faces in fear, praying for the attack to stop. Yona opened his jaw and pounced on Silas Barnett. A cloud of darkness swallowed the man and spread quickly through the entire town. It was so black that no one could see more than a foot in front of them. The townsfolk crouched in fear, shaking and praying to their own God.

Then suddenly, as quickly as it had appeared, it began to lift and dissipate. And just like that, the storm was over.

There was no more shooting, no more lighting, no more thunder, no more screaming. The drums were still beating, but the people felt safe enough to lift their heads and come out of hiding. They migrated into the street. Silas was gone, and his gun lay in the dirt. The clouds had broken up that quickly and floated off, leaving the sky bright with stars. The church was now dark, but there was still a faint white light coming from the edge of the trees.

The people came together in the center of town. Edward was still on his knees chanting. Diana ran to Ben. They all wanted to ask questions but knew that no one there could answer them. So, they stood quietly and looked into the light in the trees. Figures began to take shape at the edge of the light and walk out of the trees, but somehow, no one was frightened by them at all. They all stood quietly watching. Hundreds of people appeared, and in the center of the group was a beautiful pregnant woman with long dark hair. She smiled to Xuan and outstretched both her hands. The little girl began to cry and ran to her mother. She grabbed hold tightly and wrapped her arms firmly around her legs, as if she was never going to let go again. The drums continued as the light became brighter and whiter until the townspeople once again could no longer look straight into it. Then it slowly receded back into the trees and faded away, taking the figures with it. The night became eerily silent and dark.

For a long time, the people of Willow Springs stood and said nothing. They just stared into the forest as it faded back to darkness. No one spoke. Edward rose to his feet. Diana hugged Ben tightly. Several men helped Mr. Ferguson to his feet, placed him into a pickup truck, and headed down to the city hospital.

Slowly and quietly, the people of Willow Springs drifted back into their homes. No one spoke.

In the morning, the sun rose and crossed the bedroom as it had each previous morning. Diana lay in the bed for a while, thinking about the night before. *Was that a strange dream? Was it real? Where is Ben?* She sat up, ready to call out his name when the door opened. Ben appeared smiling, with two cups of coffee.

"What a night," he joked. "I didn't think that you would be awake yet."

She pulled back the blankets on his side of the bed so he could sit with her. She really was grateful for the coffee. She drank a few sips, and they both sat quietly for a moment. Then she put her hand on top of his. "Did that really happen last night?" she asked, even though she knew the answer.

He put his arm around her and pulled her close. "We are alright now, honey."

"How do we tell anyone back home about any of this?" she asked. "I mean, it is so unreal."

"Honestly, Diana, I can't imagine it. It has only been a few weeks that we have been here, but it seems like our lives in Lancaster were so long ago. I cannot even imagine going back there."

Diana did not argue. She leaned back and drank her coffee. She knew he was correct. The experience that they had shared with the townsfolk had forever changed who they were as people and what they believed. Through their experiences here, Ben and Diana had bonded with the town in a way that few communities ever do anymore. They both knew that this was where they belonged. She smiled to her husband. "It appears that Willow Springs finally has a new doctor."

Ben took the mug from her and set it on the table. He tilted her head back and kissed her deeply. He slid his legs up onto the bed and rolled toward her. Just then, Barley began to scratch at the door and bark. Diana laughed. "Really, he needs to go out now?"

www.ingramcontent.com/pod-product-compliance
Lightning Source LLC
Chambersburg PA
CBHW070618310726
48982CB00001B/111

9781951985707